THE
FINAL
RECONCILIATION

ALSO BY
TODD KEISLING

THE SOUTHLAND MYTHOS

The Sundowner's Dance
Devil's Creek
Scanlines

THE MONOCHROME TRILOGY

A Life Transparent
The Liminal Man
Nonentity

COLLECTIONS

Ugly Little Things: Collected Horrors
Cold, Black & Infinite: Stories of the Horrific & Strange

PRAISE FOR THE WORK OF TODD KEISLING

"Todd Keisling is a born storyteller, drawing the reader into artfully constructed narratives that scout the darker end of the literary spectrum with skill and bravado. A pleasure to read, his stories linger well after the last page has been turned. Excellent stuff." —JOHN LANGAN, author of *The Fisherman*

"Todd Keisling is already a mainstay of modern horror, and this book proves why. A wildly original and unsettling tale, *The Sundowner's Dance* is an unforgettable journey of grief, cosmic horror, and making the most of the time we've got left. Pick up a copy of this book immediately." —GWENDOLYN KISTE, Bram Stoker Award®-winning author of *Reluctant Immortals* and *The Haunting of Velkwood*

"Filled with anxiety, anguish, and grief, *Cold, Black & Infinite* tips, bends, and spins reality. This is Keisling at his best." —CYNTHIA PELAYO, Bram Stoker Award®-winning author of *Loteria* and *The Shoemaker's Magician*

"The author has a keen, lucid understanding of suffering, which lends each plot-line extra heft and depth. These stories contain tenderly and humanely rendered characters who are drawn towards various forms of uncanny annihilation. After reading this excellent collection, I'm eagerly awaiting whatever Keisling produces next." —JON PADGETT, author of *The Secret of Ventriloquism*

"Todd Keisling's *The Sundowner's Dance* is a harrowing work of cosmic horror that masterfully inhabits a dark territory somewhere between John Langan and Bentley Little. Highly recommended." —BRIAN KEENE, author of *The Rising*

"Keisling is a cosmic cartographer forging through the darkest depths of our nightmares. He is a bard of the abyss, a voice from the void, and the horrors he's charted within this unforgettable collection will change the literary map for generations to come." —CLAY MCLEOD CHAPMAN, author of *Wake Up and Open Your Eyes*

"*Cold, Black & Infinite* is a compelling cocktail of American folklore, gothic hauntings, and urban myth, served up with Keisling's consummate flair and garnished with a swirl of blood. Resounds with everyday terror." —LEE MURRAY, four-time Bram Stoker Award®-winning author of *Grotesque: Monster Stories*

"*Devil's Creek* is the kind of book you have to read with your lights on. Hell, make sure your neighbors have their lights on too!" —S. A. COSBY, *New York Times* bestselling author of *Razorblade Tears* and *Blacktop Wasteland*

"Make no mistake. This is no imitation. This is original, fierce, and explosive writing [...] Keisling is a master storyteller." —ERIC LAROCCA, author of *Things Have Gotten Worse Since We Last Spoke*

"Reading *The Sundowner's Dance* is a bit like casting a spell to ward off existential dread despite the greatest terrors of the novel evoking this very thing; the beauty and hopefulness at the core of the story refuse to be stamped out by either the wrath of an alien invader or the ravages of age. It's Todd Keisling at his absolute finest: dark, unflinching, visceral, and innovative. His pitch-perfect prose and masterful storytelling will leave you, quite literally, breathless." —CHRISTA CARMEN, Bram Stoker Award®-winning and Shirley Jackson Award-nominated author of *The Daughters of Block Island*

THE
FINAL
RECONCILIATION

 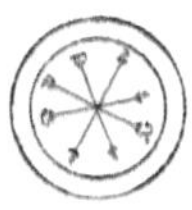  

TODD
KEISLING

Crystal Lake Publishing
www.crystallakepub.com

This story is dedicated to the memory of Greg Tompkins, a talented musician who left us far too soon.

I didn't get to say goodbye, so this will have to do.

This one's for you, brother.

*"Songs that the Hyades shall sing,
Where flap the tatters of the King,
Must die unheard in
Dim Carcosa."*

"Cassilda's Song" *The King in Yellow*, Act 1: Scene 2

THE
FINAL
RECONCILIATION

LINER NOTES

THE YELLOW KINGS PRESENT

THE FINAL
RECONCILIATION

1 - RECONCILIATORY MATTERS
2 - THE WANDERER ON DARKENED SHORES
3 - LOST IN DIM CARCOSA
4 - THE USURPER'S ASCENT
5 - SEASON OF THE LEECH
6 - BENEATH BLACK STARS
7 - BEHIND PALLID MASQUES
8 - THE FINAL RECONCILIATION
9 - TATTERS OF THE KING

THE YELLOW KINGS ARE:

JOHNNY LEIFTHAUSER (VOCALS & RHYTHM GUITAR)
AIDAN CROSS (LEAD GUITAR)
HANK JONES (BASS)
BOBBY STONE (DRUMS & SYNTH)

MANAGEMENT:
REGGIE ALLEN

SPECIAL THANKS:
CAMILLA BIERCE

TRACK #1
RECONCILIATORY MATTERS

 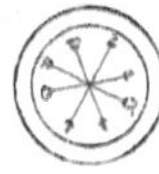  

Miles Hargrove peered at the old man through a curtain of cigarette smoke. The lights in the community room were turned down at the aging rock star's request, but he still wore sunglasses, and Miles realized he could see the cameraman's reflection in them.

"Jody," the producer said, snapping his fingers. "Can we get a different angle?"

Aidan Cross sat back in his seat while the producer sought a better shot. He sucked down the first cigarette in two long drags and chuckled when the thought occurred to him: *Maybe this is what Keith Richards felt like.*

Keith was dead, though. Had been for years. He'd shuffled off to that long-lost Valhalla to spend eternity drinking wine off the tits of beautiful women.

Aidan had never met Keith Richards, but he liked to think they would've gotten along. Not that it mattered now.

The producer, Miles, turned back to his interview subject. "Apologies, Mr. Cross. The low lighting is causing some difficulties. We should be ready in just a few moments."

"No worries," Aidan mumbled. "It's your dime, kid."

Miles Hargrove offered a smile that reminded Aidan of their old manager, Reggie Allen. Reggie used to smile like that all the time before his face was torn off. Old Reggie's smile was never quite the same after that.

Jody repositioned the camera and gave Miles the okay with his thumb and forefinger. The producer sat up and leaned forward. He gave Aidan another liar's smile.

"We're just about ready to start," he said, "and before we do, Mr. Cross, I just want to say that I've been a big fan of yours for a long time. I used to play a little guitar back in college, and your songs were always a favorite with the ladies. The Yellow Kings were my favorite band back then."

Aidan sat back in his chair and lit another cigarette. For a moment his face was set alight from the spark, illuminating the scars that stretched across his haggard face. He spoke with a voice full of gravel and ash. "What changed?"

The smile fell away from the producer's face. "Pardon?"

"We were your favorite *back then*. What changed?"

"Well, after all that happened… I—"

Aidan Cross raised his hand and smirked. "Relax, Mr. Hargrove. Are we rolling?"

Miles nodded. "We are. Feel free to start any time."

The old rock star leaned forward, planting his bony arms on the table and clasping his hands as if in prayer. Long, lazy tendrils of smoke rose from the cigarette's cherry, shrouding the room in a dull haze. The way the light filtered through that smoggy cloud gave Aidan an inhuman glow. Jody had done his best to capture the old man's good side, but the years had been unkind, and in this light, he could not tell where the wrinkles stopped and the scars began.

"You know, Mr. Hargrove—"

"Miles. You can call me Miles."

"—Miles, then. I only agreed to this interview for one reason."

"And what reason is that?"

Aidan reached up and pulled the sunglasses down the bridge of his nose. Miles blinked, fighting back the urge to look away from the puckered scars lining the old man's eyes. The stories about what happened that night did those scars no justice; they were hideous things, cavernous in Aidan's sagging flesh, each groove the width of a fingernail that traced a map of agony down his cheeks.

Miles Hargrove swallowed back what little saliva he could muster. "It must have been horrible, what happened to you."

"I've spent the last fifty years trying to reconcile that night, Miles. I haven't had a choice—every time I look in the mirror I'm reminded of what we did. It was supposed to be the best night of our lives, but now I'm all that's left…" His lower lip quivered erratically. He pushed the shades back up to his eyes.

"Why don't you start at the beginning, Aidan?"

Aidan sighed and shook his head. "It started with the wanderer, the woman calling herself Camilla, although I don't think that was her real name. She was our undoing. I'd like to think I saw it coming, but in those days I was just as lost in her mystique as Johnny. Christ, I've not thought about him in a decade." He screwed up his face, fighting back the pulling tides of emotion, and smoked the cigarette down to its filter in a single drag. "These days I prefer not to."

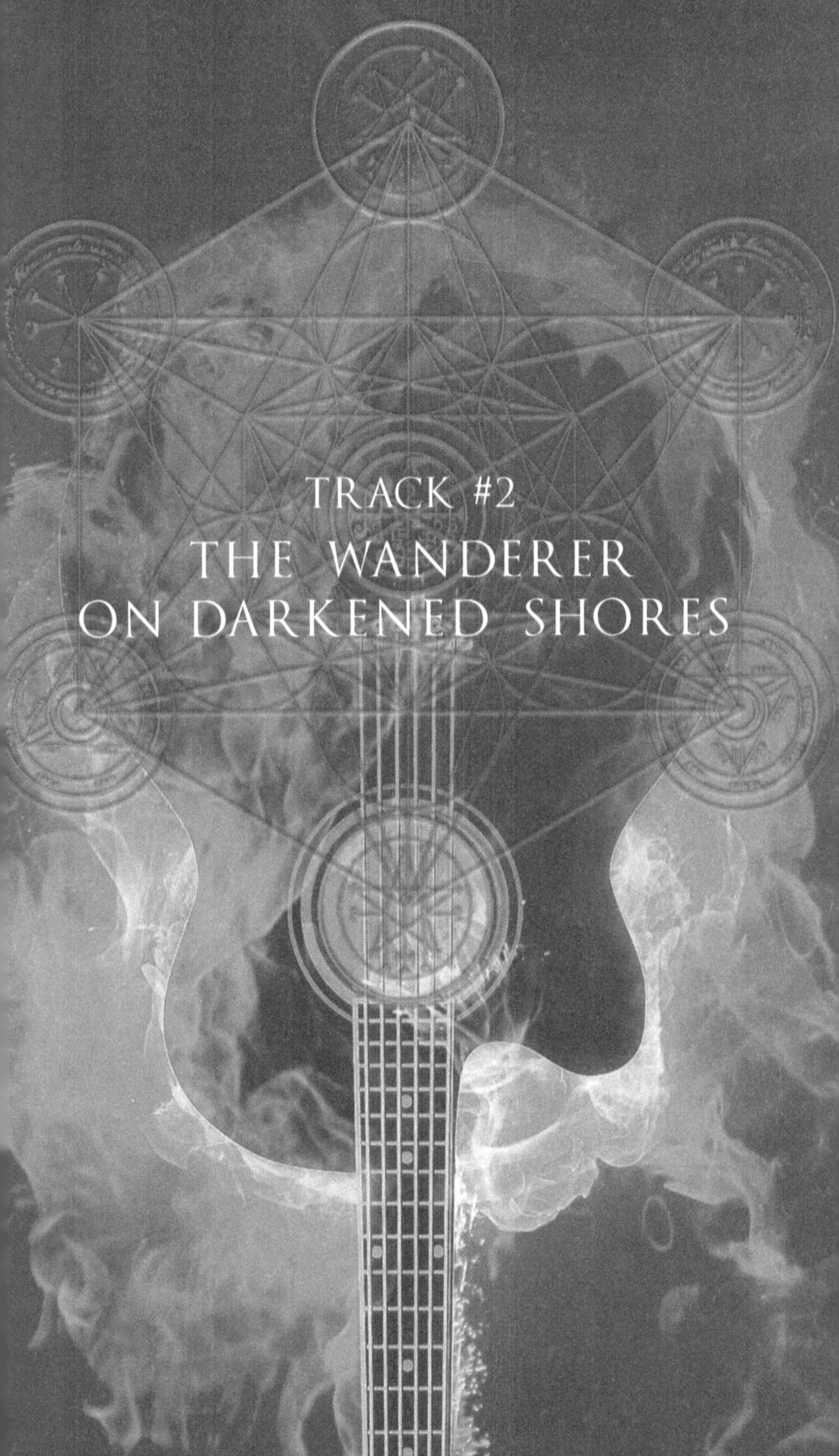

TRACK #2
THE WANDERER
ON DARKENED SHORES

Under whose black stars
do you lie?

Where are we going?
What have you done?

A handful of dust
to blot out the sun

His kingdom of gold
to defy

 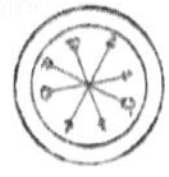  

The first time I saw Camilla Bierce was in a dive bar called Murphy's, the local watering hole in some no-name town out West. We were on tour then, supporting the *Jesters in Our Court* EP. It was our first official release, save for a self-titled demo we'd circulated to all the labels a year before. Most of the songs from that demo—'The Infernal Machination' and 'Holes in the Fabric' parts one and two, in particular—ended up on the EP, except this time they didn't sound like they were recorded in Bobby's basement.

The suits at the label were cautiously optimistic at best. Our style of rock was a niche genre for sure—no one wanted 15-minute epic rock journeys anymore, and they hadn't for at least 30 years—but other bands like Tool, Mastodon, and Opeth had found their audience, and our manager Reggie was able to convince the suits to send us on a small tour.

"Let them get their feet wet," he told them, or at least that's what he told us he told them. We weren't there for the actual meeting. Our bassist, Hank, was the only one of us who had a car, and the night before he'd gotten drunk and left his headlights on. Reggie made something up to explain our absence, but I don't remember what it was.

Anyway, Reggie was the only one who didn't seem surprised by the label's decision to pony up the cash for a tour.

"Me and a couple of the execs go way back," he said. "Besides, you boys are the full package in spades. You've got the name, the mystique, you've got the look, and more importantly you've got the *sound*. You're King Crimson two-point-oh!"

Johnny was the one who picked the name 'The Yellow Kings'. He'd lifted it from some book he read when he was in high school. He was always into weird shit like that. I think if he hadn't picked up a guitar and fallen in love with Robert Plant, he would've been one of those creepy writer dudes, sitting in the dark, hunched over a keyboard, writing about the apocalypse.

I'd like to say our 'mystique' was something we'd planned, but the truth is, all of us were pretty terrified of playing in front of a crowd. We dealt with it in our own ways. Hank always carried a bottle of Jack onstage with him. Me and Bobby, we grew our hair long to hide our faces. Johnny would always sing with his eyes closed until someone told him to just wear sunglasses like Al Jourgensen or Layne Staley. He did, and he caught a lot of flak for it at first. We joked once that maybe we should all just wear masks like the guys from Slipknot, but Reggie shot that down real quick.

You know, thinking back on it, I can see why the label wanted us to get our feet wet. We were all pretty green.

So, Reggie booked us some shows, and Bobby borrowed some money from his ma so we could buy a beat-up shit-heap of a van. And off we went, The Yellow Kings on our first tour.

We'd played live plenty of times, but always local shows or festivals, and never on our own. I think that made the stage fright easier, knowing there were other bands going through the same sort of thing. You'd be amazed how many people throw up before show time.

That first tour—what Bobby lovingly referred to as the

'Court Jesters' tour—was like going to war. It was our way of learning how to handle being on the road, performing night after night, dodging bottles, and handling hecklers. The first few shows we were timid as shit and the crowd could smell it on us. Some places, it's amazing we got out of them alive.

This one night, down in Texas, Hank's bass kept cutting out. This was before we had our own roadies to take care of shit for us, so we're halfway through our opening number—which was entirely bass-driven—and out it goes. The booing started almost instantly. One thing led to another and before we knew what was happening, Hank dives fists-first off the stage and into the crowd. We called him "Axl" for a while after that.

There we were, a bunch of no-name rednecks from the South, going out on stage every night to educate the masses with our brand of rock. Some places were more receptive than others, and they let us know it. We were lucky if we made it through a show without any bruises or cuts, but little by little, word started to spread. We knew things were starting to take off when we started selling out of shirts and CDs at our merch booth.

The night we met Camilla was our first sold out show. We were just a month into our tour, and Reggie already had to place our second rush order for more shirts and discs. Driving our shitty van around the front of Murphy's, seeing how people were already lined up outside, three hours before the show—y'know, I think that's when it really hit me things were starting to move for us.

We'd played some shitty shows before—what band hasn't?—but the good ones always stand out, and that night at Murphy's was, in my mind, one of our top five performances. Sure, the venue was complete shit, but we were on fire that night. The crowd was so energized you could feel electricity coming off them in waves, man.

Johnny hit all the right notes, my guitar stayed in tune, Hank's bass didn't cut out, and Bobby's synth actually worked this time. Trust me, trying to play 'The Infernal Machination' without the synth solo after the second chorus completely cuts the balls off that song.

The woman was waiting for us outside our van after the show. I guess you might say she was our first groupie; you could also say she was our Yoko Ono, but I'll get to that.

She was leaning against the hood, arms crossed, wearing a leather jacket, black mini-skirt, and knee-high boots. Her auburn hair spilled over her shoulders, setting her jacket alight. She had a great figure—that much, I can't deny—but the first thing I noticed was her eyes. They were different colors, like Bowie. One brown and one hazel. *Complete Heterochromia iridum*, they call it.

"Great show," she said. Her voice was like silk. "You're Aidan, right?"

I nodded, fishing the pack of cigarettes from my pocket. I stuck one in my mouth. "Smoke?" I asked.

"Of course." She plucked a cigarette from the pack. I lit it for her, and then my own. "Love your sound. That solo at the end of 'Holes' gives me chills in all the right places."

I smiled and blew a ring of smoke. "Thanks," I said. "You from around here? You don't sound Texan."

"Texan?"

"Yeah, you know. There's no Texas twang in your voice."

She laughed at that. Genuine or not, it didn't matter; that laugh of hers had a way of cutting the ice with precision. Camilla was like that, you know. She could make you feel at ease no matter the situation, like you'd been friends for years, like she'd always known you.

"No," she said finally, "I'm not from around here. I guess I'm…from all over."

"Little bit of everywhere?"

Camilla smiled. "And a little bit of nowhere."

We let some air into the conversation. I think she paused for effect, but me, I was still trying to wrap my swimming mind around that. She was being elusive, cryptic, qualities which I came to learn were common for her. Camilla had this way of spinning a conversation off the beaten path, sometimes speaking forthright, other times in riddles, and looking at you from the corner of her eye. Sizing you up. Reading you. Everyone was an open book to her. I didn't catch all of this that first time—by the time I figured her out, I was too late. And how could I? I was still buzzing from the amazing show we'd just played.

Johnny, on the other hand… Poor Johnny. Being the enigmatic, moody frontman pretty much entitled him to droves of women throwing themselves at him on an almost nightly basis, but even he was taken aback by Camilla's charm. I don't know how else to describe it, really. Talking to her for an extended period of time made you feel drunk on life, almost euphoric, like you'd just done a line of the best coke on the planet. She had that effect on all of us, but none so much as Johnny.

The moment he stepped out of the club, his shades still pulled down over his eyes, Camilla turned her attention from me and almost glided across the alley to meet him. I might as well have not even been there. At the time I wasn't at all surprised by her being there, waiting for Johnny like that. And why wouldn't she? Johnny was the one with the words and the voice of the Kings.

I know now that's exactly why she was waiting for him. She needed a voice.

They must've flirted for a good ten minutes, long enough for me to smoke two cigarettes and for Hank and Bobby to spill out the back of the club with their gear. When I was finished, I crushed the cigarette on the pavement and put my hand on his shoulder.

"Help us load up the van, would you?"

He still wore his shades, so I couldn't tell where he was looking. Probably at Camilla, who was still fawning over him, practically glowing in the dim alley light.

Johnny lifted his sunglasses and smiled. "Sure," he said, before turning back to her. He put a finger to her lips. "Hold that thought. Don't go anywhere."

"Don't worry," Camilla said. "I wouldn't leave you for anything in the world."

And she didn't. Not when we packed up our van. Not when we left town. Not when we left the state to our next gig. She came along with us, sleeping with Johnny in the back. None of us ever took a vote. Matter of fact, I can't exactly recall a single time we ever did discuss Camilla's presence on the road. It just seemed like she belonged there, and not just at Johnny's side, either. She was with all of us, in her own way. At least, I think she tried to be. Some of us wouldn't let her, but I'll get to that in a minute.

Anyway, that's how things went for the next couple of weeks, our quartet now an unofficial quintet, playing gigs at hole-in-the-wall venues every couple of days, every show sold out, Reggie scrambling to get more merchandise on order. Every night Camilla kissed each of us on the cheek before we went on stage, in a kind of sweet ritual. "For luck," she told us, "not that you need it."

And we didn't. We blew the doors off every place we played. Every night we took a bow together on stage, every night we piled back into the van, and every night Camilla came along for the ride.

One night, we were driving somewhere through Arizona, having just played our last gig of the tour in Phoenix. We were due in Los Angeles the following morning for a meeting with Reggie, and based on our GPS, we were going to be about two hours late. Par for the course, but there I was, trying to make up time by breaking the law, going thirty miles over the legal limit. The boys were asleep in the back. It was just me and Camilla and the night. We hadn't been able to pick up a decent radio station in an hour, and I was beat.

Camilla kept me focused, talking so I wouldn't fall asleep. I asked her once, sort of joking, sort of not, if she was just using us to hitchhike across the country, if she had someplace to go, and she told me, "No, I'm just a wanderer." She twirled a strand of her hair around her finger and put her feet up on the dashboard. She rolled down her window a crack, letting the cool night air into the van's cabin, kissing our faces. I shot a glance at her, and she was smiling at me.

"A wanderer, huh?"

"That's right," she said. "Your wanderer, roaming across these darkened shores of the heart."

I'd seen her swallow a pink pill with a smiley face painted on it about an hour before, so I knew she was probably tripping. Smirking, I asked her what she meant by that. She turned around in her seat and reached her hand over, trailing her fingers across my thigh.

"I want to help you take off your mask."

"My mask?"

She leaned over and whispered in my ear. "We're all wearing pallid masks."

At first, I wasn't sure what she was doing—I was driving, after all, and half asleep at that. Her words slurred together, wet with a kind of delirium that kissed my ears and put me into a sort of trance.

She'd already fished me out of my pants and had me worked into a bar of iron before I stopped her. I don't know what happened, how it happened, how I let her go that far. That part of my memory is forever gone from me. What I do know is that when I snapped out of the trance, I found my best friend's girlfriend giving me a handy while he slept mere feet away.

I shook my head. "Need you to stop that, darlin'."

"Nuh uh," she cooed. "I don't think you do."

She was right. I didn't. What she was doing with her hand felt great, and I felt myself slipping further backward into that dreamy desert place. My eyes were open, my hands on the steering wheel, but my mind was pulled back with every rise and fall of her hand. She worked at me, taking my breath away, and somewhere in the back of my mind, I heard my own voice screaming back to me to stop her, that this wasn't right, she was my best friend's girl. I glanced down at her, and her eyes weren't different colors anymore. Her eyes were yellow-gold like an animal, and they were burning holes right through me.

"You want this," she whispered, the flirtatiousness all but gone from her voice. There was someone else talking through her now, a low grating voice that had crawled up from her throat. It was wet and dark and deeply guttural, speaking words coated in phlegm, and the mere sound made me wilt in her hand. "You want this because we will it," she growled. "And we will have this because we want it."

She squeezed me tightly in her fist. Pain shot up through my groin, but I'd lost the voice to cry out. I clenched my teeth and white-knuckled the steering wheel.

"You belong to us now, and when we wish it, you *will* take off your mask. So shall you all."

A coyote darted in front of the van, and my instincts took over, but only because she allowed them to. I jerked the wheel and swerved to avoid the mangy animal. The guys in the back cried out as they were jostled from their sleep, and Camilla fell away from me, striking her head against the side of the cab.

I righted the van, guiding it off the median and back onto the highway. Dazed, my heart racing, I remembered my cock was still hanging out of my shorts, so I tucked myself back in before anyone else could notice. Camilla shook her head, giggling quietly to herself.

"Aidan, what the fuck, dude?"

Hank leaned forward and punched my shoulder.

"Sorry," I said. "Coyote. Go back to sleep."

Camilla was still laughing. I looked over at her and frowned. "That wasn't funny."

She looked at me and shrugged. She giggled for another twenty minutes before the drugs got the best of her, and she slipped into a deep sleep.

I've replayed that incident in my head multiple times a day for the last fifty years, and every day I reach the same conclusion: I should've done what I wanted to do in that moment.

I should've reached over, opened the door, and kicked her pretty ass out into the desert night. God damn me for doing nothing. God damn me for waiting until it was too late.

TRACK #3
LOST IN DIM CARCOSA

WE GAVE OUR LIVES AT
THE FOOT OF HER GOLDEN GATES

CARCOSA IS CALLING ME

CARCOSA IS CALLING ME

WE SHED OUR SKINS ON
THE BANKS OF THE HYADES

CARCOSA IS CALLING ME

CARCOSA IS CALLING ME

 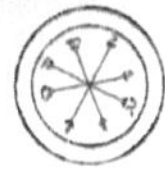  

Most of us had never been to Los Angeles before. I know it was Johnny's first time, and for Bobby and Hank that tour was their first time journeying farther west than the Mississippi. Personally, I'd only ever been to Los Angeles once when I was a kid, on a family trip to Disney, and it was about the same as I remembered it: smoggy, the sky painted a permanent yellow haze, with traffic backed up on the highway for as far as the eye can see.

The place was nothing at all like the movies had led us to believe. The whole goddamn city was a temple built to honor the nameless gods of greed and excess, a money machine that chewed up kids and shit them out every hour. For every star it birthed, ten more were damned to wander the streets and alleys, peddling their bodies for God knows what.

And there we were, four southern boys lost in the wilderness. Calling it a culture shock was an understatement.

The only one of us who wasn't enchanted by the promise of this yellow-gold Shangri-La was Camilla. As we left the freeway and made our way downtown to the record label, she was quick to point out the sights—this movie was filmed on that corner, that place had great Thai, a good place to score weed is down that street, shit like that. I wondered if she ever lived there, if that's where she came from, which makes sense in a weird sort of way.

Only a city as fake as Los Angeles could produce a creature like Camilla Bierce.

We never talked about what happened the night before, and in the days to come I wrote it off as me being too tired and her being too doped up. I wish I'd said something to Johnny. Maybe he would've knocked my teeth out, but more probably, he would've ditched her there in LA. And maybe that would've been the best for all of us. Wait. No, I know it would've been best. Not that it matters now. Things never work out the way you want them to. The Stones wrote a great song about that.

Anyway, we spent two days in the city, but we never really left that dim Carcosa. That's what Camilla called it, you see. She never said 'Los Angeles' or 'LA'. It was always Carcosa to her. She guided us along its darkened shores as the morning sun painted the horizon a cloudy gold.

Fifty years on, I still wake up at night drenched in sweat, my heart thumping like someone beating on a door, terrified that I'm still back there in my hotel room. Terrified that I'm trapped in Carcosa.

Whenever I look in the mirror at the lines on my face, I think I still am.

"Christ, you boys let Aidan drive you into town? What, you got a death wish or something?"

Reggie met us in the lobby. The record label was headquartered in a swanky office building downtown. The office was sleek and minimal, made up to look like no one occupied the place, every surface waxed so clean you could see your face in the marble. It's the sort of area that could double as an operating room, it was so fucking sterile.

I shrugged off Reggie's jab and gave the old bastard a hug. He'd been good to us, making sure we had enough merchandise and money to get from gig to gig on that tour. He was one of the first to believe in us, and I trusted him. Why I didn't listen to him about Camilla is beyond me. Maybe she'd already cast her spell on me. Surprise handjobs will do that, I suppose.

He greeted the rest of us with smiles and handshakes and hugs, but he paused when he saw Camilla. I'll never forget the look on Johnny's face when old Reggie turned back to us and said, "You boys pick up a stray?"

Johnny took off his sunglasses—he'd been wearing them almost nonstop on the last leg of the tour—and struggled to meet Reggie's stare like a scolded child.

"This is Camilla," he mumbled. "She's a friend of the band. Cam, this is Reggie, our manager."

Camilla's ruby lips were already peeled back into a smile, her face almost glowing with a false sense of happiness. Whatever charms she had, she'd turned them up to eleven for old Reggie. She held out her hand.

"Such a pleasure to meet you, Reggie. I've heard so much about you."

Now old Reggie, he'd been around the block more than once in this business. You name a band dynamic, and chances are he'd seen it. Hell, just look at your history of rock. Look at the Beatles or Nirvana, Yoko Ono or Courtney Love. You introduce a variable into an otherwise balanced equation and it tips the scales. Reggie only needed one look at Camilla and he'd already made up his mind, her charms be damned.

He was still a man of class, though. He took her hand and shook. "Pleasure's all mine, Ms. Camilla. I've not heard a thing about you, but I'm sure your man here will remedy that." The air in the room was sucked away with his words, and we all stood there staring at our shoes like we'd just let down our old man. He wasn't mad at us, per se, but man he was disappointed. Finally, Reggie broke the ice and clapped his hands.

"The gentlemen upstairs are eager to hear about your tour. I think you're going to be pleased about the things they have to tell you. Very pleased. Shit, I'm excited for you boys."

Reggie ushered across the lobby, but paused mid-step and shot a glance at Camilla.

"I'm afraid you'll need to stay down here, miss." His flabby cheeks went red, but his words didn't miss a beat. "This is a business meeting, I'm sure you understand."

"Oh, don't worry about that," Camilla said, smiling through a gaze of knives. "I'll wait down here. You guys take as long as you need. Oh, and Johnny?"

Our introverted frontman turned on his heel like a soldier given an order. Bobby snickered quietly to himself, and Hank jabbed an elbow into his ribs. Even I remember rolling my eyes at how ridiculous his reaction was. She'd been with us, what, a month? Six weeks at most? And already she had his balls tied around her finger.

Camilla swung her arms around him, pulled him close, and sucked his face for a good two minutes. The rest of us stood there, annoyed and impatient, while this guy we'd known for years let a total stranger dominate him. It was more than uncomfortable to watch; it was sickening. Not so much because of the display of affection, but because of how willingly he'd given himself to her. That wasn't the Johnny we knew. It certainly wasn't the hard-nosed quiet guy we'd grown up with.

Before she finished with her performance—and really, that's all this was, a fucking performance—Camilla locked eyes with Reggie, and I swear I saw the hint of a smile at the corner of her ruby lips. That look said everything it needed to: *This one's mine. This one belongs to me.* And he did. We just didn't know it at the time.

When she was finished, Camilla tousled Johnny's hair and gave him a quick peck on the cheek.

Her display of power concluded, Camilla left us to our business. "Good luck," she cooed. Johnny turned back to us with a puzzled look on his face, like he was in the twilight hours of a magnificent bender.

I can count on one hand all the times I ever saw Reggie spooked. That moment was one of them. The rest…well, I'll get to that.

Business meetings with the suits at the label were about as exciting as you might imagine. There were a lot of numbers, sales data, marketing plans, the whole nine. We sat there in a stupor, nodding and laughing at the right moments, letting Reggie speak for us. In a nutshell, the *Jesters in Our Court* EP was selling well. *Incredibly* well, to hear the suits talk about it, setting new sales records for the label.

Radio stations had adopted the song 'Holes in the Fabric' as an unofficial single, much to our dismay, since it was the second song of a two-parter, but our unhappiness over that fact didn't last very long. People were actually calling in to radio stations to request our song. *Our* song. That *we* wrote together. Can you believe it?

We couldn't. Not then.

The meeting concluded with an offer: a two-album deal, a generous royalty agreement, and support for a national tour. There was no hesitation on our part. We signed it willingly, happily, and celebrated that night by throwing a massive party in our hotel rooms. Why wouldn't we? It was one of the best days of our lives, everything we'd worked so hard for as a band.

I remember asking Johnny, as we rode back down the elevator after the meeting, if he thought he could write enough songs for two albums. He turned to me, in that sort of half-sleepy, half-creepy way of his, and smirked.

"I've already started writing it," he said. He put on his shades and pushed them up the bridge of his nose. "It's really quite special. Our first album is going to raise the bar pretty fucking high, my friend."

He was right. It did, but for all the wrong reasons. We never recorded that second album. The first one was enough for a lifetime.

Our wonderful manager treated us to dinner at the hotel later that night. Alcohol flowed freely during the meal, so much that Bobby had a hard time with his lobster claws. I'm not sure if he'd ever had lobster before that night, so he was probably lost to begin with. Watching him try to drunkenly extract the meat of the claw was the cause of much laughter, so much that the hotel manager asked us twice to keep it down. Not that we gave a shit.

So about that party I mentioned. I don't remember whose idea it was to get shitfaced, but none of us—including Reggie—had a problem with it. Old Reg covered the tab that night, ordering round after round at the hotel bar. We started out with beers, graduated to shots, and about there is where the night gets hazy for me.

Here's what I remember: Hank spilling his Irish Car Bomb all over Johnny's vintage Rage Against the Machine T-shirt (*I bought that on their last fucking tour, you dick!*); Reggie sermonizing about the good old days to Bobby, who was so blitzed out of his mind that every other word out of our manager's mouth was a comedic revelation; Johnny sulking over a whiskey on the rocks, and I'm unclear if he was just being his usual brooding self or if he was upset over the spilled drink; and Camilla sitting beside him, braiding a strand of her hair with his.

I remember staring at her while she did, partially because I wasn't sure what I was witnessing. At the time I thought it was one of the dumbest fucking things I'd ever seen. It was some high school-level shit, you know? Was she going to wear his class ring next?

But thinking on it now, I think I was mystified by what she was doing. Sure, I was drunk, I fully admit that part, but I do remember that part of the night with clarity. Johnny seemed oblivious to what she was doing, almost as though she wasn't even there at all. Hell, he didn't even wince when she pulled the slack out of his hair. He sat there, drinking his whiskey while she twisted and tied a red strand of hair to his. The whole thing had the feeling of a ritual. I don't know how else to explain it, but it's like she was, I don't know, *binding* herself to him. Or him to her. Either way, watching her do this to him, I felt like a helpless intruder, unable to do anything to stop her and also completely uninvited to witness the event.

When she finished, she turned to me and smiled. "Isn't he cute? I think it suits him." She chewed her bottom lip and traced one finger along my arm. "Want me to do you next?"

I didn't respond to her. Instead, I got up from my seat and staggered out of the bar and back up to my hotel room. From here, things become a series of snapshots, like still images cut from a broken film.

My room was cold. The A/C was cranking away, and I stumbled over to the window to adjust the thermostat.

I fell face-first into bed. I didn't bother undressing or even turning down the sheets. There's a lot of darkness after this, and I don't remember how long I was out. All I know is that I passed out when I hit the pillow for an indeterminate amount of time, and I was somehow yanked out of my drunken slumber by a heavy knocking on my door.

Camilla was there with Johnny, Hank, Bobby, and Reggie in tow. She didn't say anything as she invited herself into my room. The other guys followed her single-file. They might as well have been strung along on a leash. I mumbled something as they sauntered in, probably asking what the hell they're doing, but none of them said anything to me.

After I closed the door, Camilla turned and snapped her fingers. "Sit there," she told them, pointing to the floor. They obeyed, sitting in unison, their chins turned downward as if in prayer.

"Guys," I slurred, "what the fuck is this?"

Camilla turned to me. Her eyes were one color again, two golden marbles set alight and blazing with an impossible fire. She licked her lips, and when she spoke she did so with the voice of many. There was more than just Camilla inside her. I know that now. Legion, some call it, but I know it by another name. It was the voice of a king. *The* king. A true king of many, unspeakable by any sane mortal tongue. We all bore his mark when we took the stage for the final time, but that night in the hotel room was the first I'd ever heard it.

"Coronation in the city of gold," Camilla said. "Together we will sing the song of the Hyades in the court of Carcosa, and you will bear the sign of Hastur the Unspeakable, his glorious majesty and the true Yellow King."

Hastur? The true Yellow King? Coronation? My head swam, my brain soaked in a pool of liquor so deep I'd spend a week treading the surface of a hangover, and all this mystical mumbo-jumbo-bullshit did was make me wish I'd had one more shot of bourbon to take the edge off. I looked at the guys, who were all lined up and pouting like scolded children. Johnny wasn't wearing his sunglasses. He was rocking back and forth, mumbling words I couldn't understand.

"Johnny?"

He paused, and when he looked up at me, my blood went cold. His eyes burned with the same golden fire. Hank, Bobby, and Reggie followed his gaze like dominos, one after the other, their eyes burning gold. One by one, they smiled, and only then did Johnny speak.

"We've been chosen, Aidan. Join us."

The world spun out of control as I backed away. I'm not sure what I was trying to accomplish. Run away, maybe, not that I would've gotten very far. My motor skills were heavily compromised, the liquor having already worked its magic. Or maybe it was her magic. I'll never know for sure, but I've long suspected Camilla's dark tricks had something to do with it. Even drunk, I could've made my way out of that room, but I didn't. The will, *my* will, was gone from me.

When I looked back at her, I felt my last ounce of resistance slip away from me, withering and dying in the gilded light of her fiery gaze.

"Shhh," she cooed. "Do not fret, child."

My knees buckled, and I sank to the floor. Tears streamed down my face. Behind us, the guys hummed and murmured together, rocking excitedly in frantic meditation.

The tips of her toes traced along the plush carpeting as she hovered toward me. Moments later, I felt her fingers work their way through my hair. She tilted my head back and our eyes met.

"The Yellow King has plans for you," she whispered. "All of you. And they begin here in this room. With me. With all of us." She tightened her grip on the back of my head. I cried out as her nails sank into my skull, guiding me forward toward her. "Now," she growled, "lick me."

I know what you're probably thinking. We all got drunk and took turns defiling our groupie. That isn't what happened. *She* defiled *us*. Our bodies, our minds. Our souls. I have scars in places you wouldn't believe.

She took turns with us, forcing the others to watch at the bedside, chanting words that didn't make sense to me. I'm not even sure they were actual words. Awful guttural sounds that hurt to utter.

We didn't talk about that night for the longest time. By the time we did, it was too late to matter. The damage had been done, Camilla's influence over us complete and absolute.

I have a recurring nightmare from time to time. My phone rings at my bedside, and when I answer it, Johnny's on the other end. He's raspy and choked because his throat is missing, and he tells me, "Aidan, where are you, brother? We need you to shred for us. The band can't practice without you."

I tell him that I'm here in the nursing home, that I haven't touched a guitar for years, and besides that, he's dead, how could he possibly sing? And then I ask him where he's calling from, and he tells me.

"We're in Carcosa now. We're getting the band back together. All we need is you."

I always wake up in a cold sweat. Nights like that are the worst. I haven't had a good night's rest since the night in the hotel. Imagine the worst hangover you can, and then imagine it never goes away. A hangover that lasts the rest of your life.

That's my life, Mr. Hargrove, and it all started that night. That night was more than just sex to her. It was a ritual in honor of her king. Whatever she did to us marked us for the rest of our lives. We lost ourselves in Carcosa that night. I don't think any of us ever really made our way back.

TRACK #4
THE
USURPER'S ASCENT

I AM THE USURPER
A THIEF IN THESE
TWILIT HOURS

HERE TO CLAIM A STOLEN
THRONE
WHILE THE MILK OF TIME
CURDLES & SOURS

Reggie was gone by the time we woke the next morning. We didn't see him again for a month, and by that point we were so wrapped up in recording the album that none of us dared bring up what happened. When we woke up in the same room together, we just figured we'd had one hell of a bender the night before, and blacked out. It wasn't the first time that had happened. For a while I had myself convinced that the blurry memories of that night were nothing more than nightmares, phantoms conjured from my subconscious by the booze.

Magical thinking, you know. I think we all knew what had happened, but were too afraid to speak of it. Losing control of yourself is a hard thing to admit. You look back and think: Hey, there's no way I could've done that. That wasn't me. That was some other guy.

But we knew the truth. That morning, Hank, Bobby, and me all booked flights back home for a short vacation. Johnny chose to stay in Los Angeles to start working on the album.

Standing in the hotel lobby, I asked him, "Do you have a place to stay?"

Camilla answered for him. "I have a place he can stay. It's quiet."

"Johnny," I said, frowning. "Take off those goddamn glasses and look at me." He did so. He looked haggard, like he hadn't slept in weeks. If I didn't know any better, I'd swear he was on something. Heroin, maybe, or some other kind of opiate, but if I knew anything about my friend it's that he didn't touch any of that shit. That's one thing the media got wrong about us after what happened. Drugs had nothing to do with it. I want to set that record straight here and now.

"You're sure about this? I mean, really sure? Things have been kind of weird lately, and—"

"Aidan," he said. "I'm good. Just tired from the road. You guys go on ahead. I'll be fine. By the time you get back, I'll be ready to work. Promise."

I didn't say anything. All I could do was nod. Camilla walked up behind him and wrapped an arm around his chest. She planted her chin on his shoulder and smiled at me. The fucking bitch even winked. It was the same look she'd given Reggie the day before, and I received that message loud and clear: *This one's mine. This one belongs to me.*

Going back home after being on the road for months was weird. We'd left our hometown without any fanfare at the start of the tour, something we expected but were no less disappointed by. I mean, how often do four kids from Stauford, Kentucky actually get signed by a record label and embark on a nationwide tour? Probably not often, but our little hometown didn't care. We were nobodies growing up there, we were nobodies when we left, and we were not at all surprised to find that we were still nobodies when we went back. Such is life in Stauford. She doesn't give a shit.

The whole flight home, I wanted to say something to Hank and Bobby about the previous night. Not only about what had happened, but about what Camilla's presence was doing to the band, and yet I found myself filled with a sense of trepidation any time I tried to speak. Even now I don't know why I didn't speak up, but given all that had happened up to that point, I wouldn't be surprised if Camilla had cast some sort of spell over us. I suspect Hank and Bobby felt the same way, their tongues held in place by the fear of what might happen if they spoke up.

Before we went our separate ways, the three of us promised to regroup in a couple of weeks. Sooner if Johnny called for us, which he did, but I'll come back to that. I think we would've left early even if he hadn't called for us. After traveling across the country and seeing what else was out there waiting for us, our hometown seemed smaller than before, if that makes sense. Or maybe we were bigger? Older, I mean. Wiser. Something like that.

In any case, everything was where we'd left it. Our folks were still pissed at us for leaving, the local government was still corrupt, the cops were still assholes, and the only real thing that had changed was the town drunk had been struck and killed by a couple of kids out joyriding one night.

Hank's folks owned the junkyard just outside of town. He was expected to take up the family business after high school, but his heart was in the band, and the night he told them he wanted to make music led to an argument of biblical proportions. Having actually gone out into the world and found some modicum of success in pursuing his passion didn't mean much to his folks. He'd abandoned them, after all. When we got back together a week later, all he said was his old man was still an asshole. Wouldn't say much more than that, but the bruise on his jaw said everything it needed to.

Out of the four of us, Bobby was the one who came from any semblance of wealth. Well, as close to wealth as you can get in a town like that. Lower middle-class, based on the rest of the country, but in that part of the world, his family lived like royalty. I admit that when we were auditioning for drummers, Bobby wasn't our first pick, but he could also play keys, and he was the only one we knew whose parents could afford to buy him a Kurzweil for his birthday. Their problem with him wasn't that he'd left town to pursue his passion, but that he'd done so with the likes of us.

As for me, my parents were somewhat more forgiving of my choice of occupation, but they still weren't pleased with my decision to abandon college in favor of going on tour. They were happy to see me when I returned home, welcoming me with open arms and treating me to dinner, but under the pretense that I'd gotten this 'rock star' thing out of my system. They were less than thrilled to learn I had no intention of going back to school. Music was my passion, and we had a good thing going for us. They didn't understand that once it's in your blood, it's there for life. Passion is passion. Besides, there were darker tides pulling me back west, even if I wouldn't admit it to myself.

The argument that ensued with my folks led to me booking a hotel for the rest of my stay. I wasn't welcome in their home anymore because I refused to pursue the future they'd planned for me, and after that first night back home I didn't speak to them again until after our final show.

We were in town for a grand total of five days when Johnny called me. I think I speak for all of us when I say we were more than a little relieved.

"Aidan?"

I looked at the hotel alarm clock, trying to decipher the time. I was still thinking on West Coast terms, and couldn't understand why the blocky red numbers read 3:00 AM.

"Yeah," I grumbled, rolling over and reaching for the lamp. "Johnny? That you, man?"

"Did I wake you?"

"No," I said. "Yeah. Doesn't matter. What's up, man? You okay?"

"Okay?" He giggled like a child. "I'm great. Never better. How's the hometown?"

"What do you think?" I reclined back against the headboard and closed my eyes. "Same old shithole. My folks threw me out. Haven't talked to Bobby or Hank, but I suppose they're not doing much better."

The phone fell silent for a moment, so long that I checked the screen to make sure we were still connected. We were. Johnny cleared his throat. "Did, uh, did you happen to swing by Ma's place?"

My stomach dropped. I hadn't. "Uh, no, man. I didn't. I'm sorry."

"No sweat, brother. I don't blame you. I wouldn't either."

That was a lie. If Johnny had come with us, he would've spent all of his time at his mother's side in the psychiatric facility. Norma Leifthauser had spent most of Johnny's childhood in and out of various institutions. There was a point during high school where it seemed like her doctors had found the right combination of meds to keep her balanced, but the night we graduated she slit her wrists. Johnny found her in the bathtub. That's what our song 'Holes in the Fabric' was really about. I guess we can put years of online speculation to rest on that one.

Anyway, in one of Norma's final lucid moments, she told Johnny to go chase his dreams. And he did. If not for Camilla, he would've flown back with us, and chances are if he had, that would've been the end of The Yellow Kings. No final show, no final album. We would've gone our separate ways, or more likely me, Hank, and Bobby would've struck out on our own. I often wonder what would've happened if things had gone that way instead. I guess I just like torturing myself.

The truth was, I'd forgotten all about Johnny's mother. Now that he'd brought it up, a sour warmth filled my gut, and I felt horrible.

"Seriously, Johnny, I'm sorry. I—"

"Aidan, it's no sweat. Honest. That's not why I called you."

His words didn't make me feel any better. That sour feeling in my stomach tightened, forming a leaden weight of guilt that anchored me to the bed.

"Okay." I frowned. "So what's up?"

"I need you guys to fly back here to Carcosa."

Carcosa. That was Camilla's word. Hearing it glide across his tongue left me unsettled. The name just sounded wrong in his voice.

"Did something happen? Is everything all right?"

"Everything is…perfect," Johnny said. The lilt in his voice, a rising octave with that last syllable, betrayed any steadiness in his voice. Johnny had this way of measuring his words and emotions, trying to appear as flat as possible in all manner of interactions, but sometimes he slipped. Whatever it was, he was *excited*. I hadn't heard him this excited since the night we signed with Reggie to manage us.

"Define 'perfect' for me, Johnny."

"Perfect is lyrics and riffs, Aidan. They're coming faster than I can write 'em down, man. I need my band. Whatever spark is there, we need to capture it while it's popping, and I can't do it without you."

I sat up in bed and wiped the fatigue from my eyes. For the first time in weeks, I felt a genuine jolt of excitement myself. Johnny's moods were infectious like that.

"No shit? Read some of them to me?"

Then he did, and I knew we had something special. An hour later I was rallying the troops, and by breakfast, me and Hank and Bobby were on our way back to the airport. The next time I visited my hometown, I'd be the lone survivor of that horrible show. The last of The Yellow Kings.

Reggie, Hank, Bobby, and Johnny would be dead.

Five days. We were gone five days, and in that time, Camilla Bierce had furthered her influence over our friend. The wanderer had worked her dark magic, commanding Johnny with a spell that the rest of us had only glimpsed that night in the hotel. I never should've left him alone with her.

Camilla's place was a loft apartment in downtown Los Angeles. Far as I could tell, she was the only occupant (besides Johnny), which made me wonder how the hell she could afford such a place. In the weeks we were together on the road, not once had she mentioned a job or a trust fund. Hell, I would've accepted lottery winnings as a valid excuse, but ultimately I didn't ask, and she didn't offer an explanation. I will say this, though: the girl had expensive tastes, and for a self-proclaimed nomad, she knew how to live like a queen.

The whole apartment was decorated in lavish art, with full-sized stone sculptures of humanoid creatures adorning the far corners, and original canvas paintings depicting various scenes of debauchery. One painting portrayed a man held upside down while two mischievous devils sawed him in half, starting with his testicles. That painting hung above the toilet.

Scenes of mutilated animals, ritualistic torture, and bizarre sex acts decorated her apartment in such a way that no matter where you turned, there was always something unsettling staring back at you. And the centerpiece of her macabre collection was found in the area she'd designated as her living room. The space was walled off with two floor-to-ceiling bookcases; the sofa was positioned to face a free-standing sculpture at the opposite wall.

The sculpture was…how can I put this, Mr. Hargrove? It was the most fucked up thing I've ever seen.

Sculpted from porcelain or maybe marble, it stood seven feet tall, draped in a robe that was expertly crafted to look like actual fabric, spilling over the contours of a body underneath. Multiple arms protruded from the abdomen, some bent at the wrong angles, some ending in hooves, and some curved inward upon themselves like snakes.

The sculpture's head looked human, but its face was obscured by one of its hands, the fingers splayed over the eyes, nose, and mouth. Upon closer inspection, the nails of each sculpted finger seemed to dig into that porcelain white flesh, the sculptor capturing this bizarre creature mere moments before self-mutilation. And in its other hand was a plain white mask. A strange, curved symbol was etched into the mask's forehead.

We were silent throughout Camilla's tour of her not-so-humble abode, but when we saw that ungodly statue, Hank broke that silence in the only way he could.

"What in the actual fuck is that?"

Camilla beamed, prancing across the living room toward the statue. She ran her fingers along its chest and looked back at us. "I commissioned this piece. Isn't he beautiful? Our King Hastur, frozen at the moment of his unmasking."

Bobby and me, we sort of mumbled our approval to be polite, but Hank just stared at it slack-jawed.

"That is the god-awfulest thing I've ever seen, darlin', and I've seen some shit."

Camilla blanched at his comment, preparing to fire back criticisms of her own, but Johnny interrupted the standoff.

"Come on, guys, let me show you what I've been working on."

We followed him into their bedroom, but before I stepped away, I took another look at the statue. Camilla stood on her toes and kissed her king's pale wrist. I thought I heard her say, "Soon, my love." She looked over her shoulder, caught my eye, and winked.

"Aidan, you coming?"

"Yeah," I said, forcing myself to look away. I joined the boys in the next room and tried to shake off the chill that had come over me.

We gave an interview for one of those self-proclaimed 'metal' magazines a couple of months before the last show. We gave several, in fact, but this one stands out in my memory because of the question we were asked.

"This album came together quickly. What was the writing process like?"

Johnny took the lead on that question, as he did with most media requests in those days, regurgitating a canned response that Camilla had probably fed him hours before.

"I'd had the lyrics swimming around in my head," he'd told the interviewer, "and the music sort of wrote itself. Like it was always there, you know? Like it was being whispered to me from afar."

Whispered from afar. The fans loved that mystical shit. It was reminiscent of Led Zeppelin's mystique, culled from Jimmy Page's fascination with Aleister Crowley. Johnny just put our spin on it. The Yellow Kings were bringing dark magic back to metal, or some dumb shit like that.

I mention this because the interviewer ate it up. They paraphrased that quote for the article byline: 'The Yellow Kings: Whisperers From Afar.' And they ate it up because, in truth, no one really *believed* it. It was our shtick, our gag, our stage theatrics like Alice Cooper or Marilyn Manson. It was another way for the label's marketing team to package our music for the masses.

But the thing is, it was absolutely true. Those lyrics were swimming around in Johnny's head and had been for as long as Camilla had been in the picture. They were being whispered to him from afar, only they weren't coming from the ether; no, they were coming from the wanderer herself. Camilla had been telling him what to say, 'inspiring' what to write on paper, right down to the melodies themselves. And the dumb bastard was so blind to her suggestions that he thought *he* was the genius of that relationship, that everything had just come to him in some bizarre flash of wisdom.

But I knew better. Maybe Hank and Bobby did, too, but were too afraid to say anything. The notes that he strummed for us in Camilla's bedroom weren't his usual style. They were cleaner, polished, but reverberating with a dark edge underneath. The sound had weight to it, the way you feel thunder in your bones during a storm. Even now, thinking about it gives me goosebumps.

When he finished, I asked him to play it again, and this time I closed my eyes. I bobbed my head to a silent beat and let my imagination take me away. I saw a city emerge from the shadows of my mind, a bright golden palace built from impossible stone structures filled with holes. Towers jutted outward at angles which made no sense, and as I stood on that far-off vista, I realized the city was moving, breathing, whispering to me. *Take off your mask*, it said. *Take off your mask.*

"So what do you think?"

I opened my eyes. The city was gone, but that hushed voice remained in the back of my mind, lurking from the shadows.

Bobby nodded. "It's got a weird timing to it, but that's not a bad thing."

"I think the bass will drive the song," Hank said. "What about you, Aidan?"

"I dig it," I said. "What're you calling it?"

Johnny smiled. "This one's called 'The Final Reconciliation.' I think the whole album will be called that."

Hank shrugged. "What the hell's that mean?"

"I'm not sure yet," Johnny sighed. He closed his eyes. "I think it's like a metaphor for unity, like bringing two worlds together. Reconciling them. One world has to see the other, but they can't yet. I don't know, I'm still working out the journey."

The journey. That was his way of saying it's a concept album. Like Rush, Mastodon, King Crimson, and a dozen others, The Yellow Kings would be telling a story with their music.

And oh, what a story it would be.

"So what do you say?" Johnny asked. "Want to pursue it?"

"I'm in," Bobby said, sticking out his hand. Johnny put his atop Bobby's.

Hank shrugged and followed suit. "I'm game."

The three of them looked at me, grinning. I hesitated for a moment, meeting each of their eyes, contemplating what I was about to do. I knew in my heart that Camilla had everything to do with Johnny's inspiration, but I couldn't kid myself—the music was good, and I dug the concept. Whatever her role was, I couldn't deny that it would be great for our music careers.

So after all that I'd seen, after all the warning signs and bizarre shit, I ignored the screaming voice in the back of my head and put my hand on theirs.

"Count me in," I said.

A week later, we began recording what would become our first and final album.

TRACK #5
SEASON OF THE LEECH

A SEASON FOR REAPING
A SEASON FOR BLEEDING
A SEASON TO STEAL
A SEASON FOR HEALING
A SEASON TO CRY
AND A SEASON TO DIE

THE LEECH IS HERE
TO DRINK US
FROM THE INSIDE

 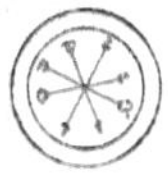  

All the rumors about the dark ritual shit that went on in the recording studio were true. Camilla had offered us free reign over her extensive book collection, an invitation which Johnny took full advantage of. I bet he carted at least thirty tomes down to the studio. They weren't top choices from the bestseller lists, either. These books were fucking ancient, dusty old things bound in cracked leather, and paper so thin it might crumble to dust if you breathed on it the wrong way.

"Grimoires," Camilla called them. Johnny was enamored immediately.

"What the hell do you need those for?" Hank asked him. We were hanging out in the control room, waiting for Bobby to finish setting up his drum kit in the studio. Johnny dropped a stack of books on the coffee table.

"Inspiration," he said.

Hank picked up one of the books and blew off a layer of dust from the cover. "Sacred geometry?" He shot Johnny a thin smile. "Don't you remember Mrs. Rice's class? You nearly failed geometry, dude."

"Not that kind of geometry, dipshit." Johnny took the book from him and flipped ahead to a marked page. "This is different. Representative of nature in all forms, seen and unseen. It all follows the golden ratio."

A diagram of something called the 'Metatron's Cube' filled the page, its thin lines stretching to the edges, bisecting one another, forming a large elaborate figure of squares, circles, and triangles. Together they completed a singular shape in which all points met in the center.

"Okay," Hank said, "so…what? Are we going to start writing songs about math? Tool already did that, man."

"No, not exactly." Johnny pointed to the Plexiglas window that looked out into the studio. Bobby was screwing his cymbals to their stands. "We're going to play in a certain arrangement."

Hank and I exchanged glances. Johnny took note of our silence, and for a moment he looked like his old insecure self from high school, still hiding behind his hair, afraid to utter a sound. That flash of insecurity made me nostalgic for better, simpler times; thinking of it now just makes me miss my friend.

He shrugged his shoulders and turned away from the window. "Trust me on this, guys. I don't know how else to explain. Just a feeling, I guess. It'll help our sound. It'll have certain acoustic properties."

I smirked. "Acoustic properties," I said. "Right."

"Are we ready to go?"

Our producer, Joe, walked into the room with a Starbucks in one hand and a notebook in the other. He'd come recommended by way of Reggie when we asked for Rick Rubin to produce the album. "Owes me a favor," Reggie had said over the phone. "He'll treat you boys right. Besides, Rubin's booked solid for two years." When we asked for Trent Reznor, he told us we couldn't afford him.

Not that it mattered. Joseph Harper was more than adequate for our production needs. Although Camilla's influence was felt throughout every step of the album's recording, Joe's presence gave it that extra punch. He took it to the next level, elevating it above just another prog rock concept record. His influence made it shine in all the right places, knowing when to smooth out Johnny's vocals or to keep my guitar's raw distortion for the master recording.

Joe was one of the few good guys involved with that record who escaped unscathed. He showed up every morning, worked with us until dinner, and called it a night. When we asked to stay behind, he showed us how to record through the studio setup. "Just enough to be dangerous," he joked. He was professional through and through, and I've nothing bad to say about him.

But enough about him. Let's get back to Johnny's weird geometry obsession.

Camilla dropped by the studio that first day to watch us set up. At first, Joe wasn't comfortable with having her in the control room, but Johnny told him to be cool, and so he was. The rest of us weren't comfortable with her there, either, but there wasn't much we could do about it. Johnny was running the show.

In our early days, there wasn't a band leader, per se. Sure, Johnny wrote the lyrics and melody, but we all contributed something to the final product. That's not to say we didn't on that record, but there was so much more involved in the recording that we had no control over. Camilla's presence, for one. Our placement in the studio, for another.

Johnny's grand plan was to have us position ourselves in each of the points of the geometric design, going as far as using rolls of green duct tape on the floor to map out a rough shape for each of the intersecting points.

"The idea," he said, "is that our creative energy and sound feed off one another. Aidan, you stand here." I followed his direction, standing midway across the studio to his right. "Hank, I want you over here."

Hank rolled his eyes and sighed like a petulant child before conforming to Johnny's vision, taking his place to the left of our singer. Bobby was positioned in the back and center, as was tradition with most band setups, with his dual Kurzweil synths off to his left.

With us in place, Johnny took the duct tape and marked our spots with green X's.

"Okay," Bobby said. "Now what?"

"Now you just keep your places when we record."

"Johnny," Hank whined. "What's the point of this? How are we supposed to see each other's cues? Seriously, man. I just want to fucking play."

"You will," Johnny said. "And just do what you normally do. All I'm asking you is to stand in a certain spot." He held out his hands in a placating gesture, but Hank was having none of it.

"Dude, all I've heard from you lately is this hippy-dippy bullshit. If you really think people are going to give a shit about religious geometry and how we're standing on the fucking stage, brother, you've got another thing coming."

I plugged in my guitar and played the opening riff to that famous Judas Priest song. Bobby and Johnny broke into a fit of laughter. Hank just shook his head and gave me the finger, but he was smiling while he did it.

A hiss of feedback broke up our reverie, and Camilla's sultry voice filled the studio. We turned back to the control room window and saw her leaning over the microphone.

"Joe wanted me to tell you time is money, boys."

Silence fell over us then. I can't speak for Hank and Bobby, but personally, I'd forgotten she was there. For that brief few minutes, we were the band again, just four friends from high school who loved music enough to try and make their own sound. We were The Yellow Kings again, and not Johnny Leifthauser's 'Trio of Jesters'. I don't know, it just felt fun again. How quickly we'd forgotten what that felt like.

Johnny blew Camilla a kiss, and I spotted Bobby rolling his eyes. He turned back to us.

"All right. 'Season of the Leech', from the top. Remember, Aidan, it starts with E. Bobby, count us down."

Bobby lifted his drumsticks.

"One, two, three, *four*—"

Other interviewers have come to me over the years to ask what it was like recording the album, if there was ever any hint that something was 'off' during the process. All of them assumed what happened was part of Johnny's 'master plan', that he actually orchestrated everything that occurred that night at our final show as fulfillment of some occult ritual. Which, in all fairness, is a legitimate assumption. How else could you rationalize such a tragedy? The media's always looking for a devil to take the blame.

The truth is, Johnny really had nothing to do with it. I can't even say it was entirely Camilla's doing.

I can see by your expression that you're surprised by my statement. Let me explain.

I've spent the last fifty years trying to wrap my brain around that period of weeks, coming to terms with what happened, how it happened, how I let things progress to that point, and so on. While I've yet to fully grasp the nature of the power of the music we made in that studio, I've come to realize Camilla wasn't the catalyst.

Sure, she manipulated us, manipulated Johnny, manipulated events in such a way that we were there at that exact time, surrounded by the right influences, but she didn't put the instruments in our hands. She didn't tell us what to play. All of us knew something was off, but the promise of success and of making more music is what drew us forward toward our fate.

All four of us chose to walk hand in hand to the gates of Carcosa. We chose to put on our masks. Some of us even chose to take them off.

But my mind wanders. The point I'm trying to get at is that we were complicit in the act of recording those songs. Camilla just had to make sure we were there every day. She made sure Johnny had the books, she kept us stocked with candles and incense for the studio, and she kept us satisfied in other ways. Johnny didn't seem to mind sharing his girl with Hank and Bobby—in fact, I think they started keeping a schedule—but I kept my distance from her. Between what had happened that night in the van and the night in the hotel room, I wanted to be as far away from Camilla as I could get.

Which wasn't very far, unfortunately. In some ways, she'd become our new manager. Reggie stayed away for most of the process. Whether he was busy or too afraid of Camilla, I'm not sure. He didn't show up again until the last couple of days of recording to listen to our progress. By then the recordings had already started to take their toll on all of us, even though we wouldn't admit it to ourselves.

I first noticed the difference a few days into the sessions. It was my turn in the studio, experimenting with a synth guitar for 'Lost in Dim Carcosa'. I'd taken my designated place, standing over the green X Johnny had left for me. Joe buzzed in over the speaker: "Just noodle for a few. I'll let you know when we have what I'm looking for."

So I closed my eyes and let my fingers play, starting with my warm-ups and moving on to more sophisticated shreds. The distorted synth effects playing back in my ears filled me with a vibration I'd not experienced since we were back in Camilla's bedroom.

You know what vertigo feels like? How you can be completely still and suddenly feel as though you're falling? Or being pulled away? It felt like that, but not quite as jarring. I didn't lose my balance, but sort of floated into the darkness as my fingers climbed the fret board.

I can't say I was really paying attention to what I was

playing. My mind was elsewhere, following darkened tides crashing against a distant shore, and somewhere on the horizon, I glimpsed the golden city once again. Its towers pierced the sky like gilded needles, filling the heavens with a brilliant light. The structures swelled and contracted, the city breathing with a hint of trepidation, waiting to welcome me into its walls. There was a congregation of figures at its gates. Tall, slender things with sickly yellow skin, their proportions elongated and distorted, as if they were drawn by a child. They wore dark red robes and blank white masks, chanting together in a low hum that made the very fabric of reality flutter around them like heat.

I'd lost myself in my music before, but this was different. I was outside myself, cognizant that I was in two places at once. I was back in the studio, eyes closed, noodling a jumble of chords on the guitar, and I was there on the shore, watching this throng of masked figures pray at the gates of an impossible city. I felt stoned. I felt elated. I felt like Dorothy gazing upon the Emerald City for the first time. I remember being amused by an idle thought, wondering if this is what Pink Floyd felt like the first time they recorded *Dark Side of the Moon*.

And then I heard the voice. The same voice I'd heard before, back in Camilla's room. It was calling to me again, carried on a warm gust of air that swept toward me in low, hushed breaths. That voice rose and fell with the tides, hissing with the spray of dark sea foam and brine, a din of ancient secrets and wisdom.

Take off your mask, it said. *Take off your mask.*

And I *wanted* to take off my mask. I wanted very badly to take off my mask, but I didn't know how. Because I wasn't wearing a mask. Because, in the back of my mind, I knew this was all a fantasy, a bizarre hallucination brought on by—what? Drugs? Booze? I was flying sober those days in the studio, so that wasn't it. Was it the music? Johnny's stupid geometry? Camilla's incense she'd left burning atop one of our amps? The candles?

The voice again, right next to me, whispering so close to my ear I could feel the breath, the trace of full lips along my earlobe. *Take off your mask, Aidan.*

A woman's voice. Not the voice of a king.

You want this. Let it happen.

Her voice. The usurper's voice. *Camilla's* voice.

I opened my eyes, and I was back in the studio, my fingers still working mindlessly along the neck of the guitar, climbing one octave after another. Joe's voice crackled through the studio intercom.

"All right, we got it. Get your Fender. I want to re-record your solo for 'Black Stars' before lunch."

We were a week into the recording when I noticed the circles under my eyes. I don't know how long they were there. I wasn't partying—none of us were—in those days. We got up for breakfast, went straight to the studio, worked until dinner, and then we went back to our hotel. Most evenings, I crashed into bed and fell into an empty, dreamless sleep.

But I felt exhausted. Like I wasn't sleeping at all. Like we were running marathons every single day we were in the studio. I wasn't the only one who looked haggard. Hank, Bobby, and even Johnny all looked worn down. Johnny looked the worst, I think. He had circles under his eyes so complete and dark we thought someone had beaten the shit out of him.

Our hands shook and our fingernails fell out. Bobby lost one of his teeth. Just fell out one night while he was eating dinner. I had bruises in odd places, along my ribs, at the tips of my elbows, and across my knuckles like I'd been punching a wall for nights on end.

One morning into the second week, Joe asked us if we were using, a question which almost got him fired.

Johnny wouldn't talk about it, but Hank and Bobby weren't as tacit about their concerns. I'll be honest with you, Mr. Hargrove: we were fucking scared. We didn't understand what was happening to us. Right up until the end, I don't think Hank or Bobby ever really understood it. Maybe Johnny did, maybe he didn't. I don't think it would've mattered one way or another. Johnny was too far gone at that point even if none of us knew it.

We could've taken a break. During our weekly conference call with Reggie, he suggested we take a weekend and drive down to Mexico, but Johnny silenced us before we could respond. "We've got a good thing going here, Reg. We don't want to mess up the mojo. You understand."

Reggie said he did, but the tone of his voice said otherwise.

"Maybe I'll pay you boys a visit," he said. "It's been too long since I saw you, and honestly, I'd love to hear the new material. I know the guys at the label are eager, too."

He meant well. He really did. We were like his kids, you know? We probably sounded ten times worse over the phone. He had every reason to worry.

After the call with Reggie, we went back to work, which is what we did every day, seven days a week. Even when Joe wasn't around, we were in the studio experimenting with different riffs and time signatures, trying to build the perfect concept album one note at a time.

This continued for a stretch of days until Bobby passed out at his drum kit one night. We were tracking the beats for 'Leech' when he just fainted right there, one arm crashing into his hi-hat with a loud hissing clang as he slumped forward over the snare. One of his drumsticks clattered dully on the throw rug below.

We were sitting at the mixing board, unsure of what had just happened. Johnny buzzed the intercom.

"What the hell. You alive in there, Bobby?"

Bobby didn't stir. The three of us got up from the board and went into the studio. Only Camilla stayed behind, reclining back on the plush couch at the opposite end of the control room. I caught a glimpse of her just before I walked out of the room. She was blowing smoke rings from her cigarette, and when she caught me looking, she flicked her tongue over her teeth and smiled.

"Better go check on Bobby boy," she said. "Looks like he drummed his little heart out."

I rolled my eyes and turned away. When I entered the studio, Johnny had successfully roused Bobby from unconsciousness. He snapped his fingers in front of Bobby's face.

"You with us, Bobby?"

Hank walked around the kit and knelt beside him. "You all right, broth—oh fuck."

Blood oozed from Bobby's left nostril, splattering in dark floral patterns on the carpet. He put his finger to his face and then stared at the blood, incredulous that something so warm and dark could be pouring out of him.

Camilla approached from behind with a box of tissues in her hand.

"At least he didn't combust," she said, plucking one of the tissues from the box and handing it to Bobby, who promptly tucked it up his nostril. We waited a few minutes while he collected himself, and the whole time I couldn't stop staring at the bloodstains on his white Bowie shirt. He loved that shirt. Now it was ruined.

Johnny was the one who started the fight. Bobby called

for a timeout to go clean himself up and to get some fresh air, but Johnny wasn't too happy about that.

"We still need to get those beats down for the mix, dude."

Bobby shook his head. "No way, man. My heart's racing and my head feels like a fucking jackhammer is at work inside it. Let me sleep and start fresh tomorrow."

When Bobby rose from his seat he took one step and staggered, shooting his arms outward to steady himself. Hank was at his side in a moment to catch him.

"See what I mean?" Bobby half-smiled, half-grunted.

Johnny shook his head. "Just five more minutes."

"He said no, John." Hank had that look in his eye, the kind every self-respecting southern boy has. The kind that says, "Don't fuck with me right now, bud." He'd also called Johnny by his given name, an act which Johnny despised, and everything pretty much escalated from there. When Camilla inserted herself into the conversation, Hank exploded.

"What's another five minutes, Bobby?"

Hank spun around and got in her face. "I don't recall asking for your opinion, bitch."

She played it off with a shrug and a smile, but Hank had had enough. Even now I admit the guy had some balls to stand up to her, especially after experiencing all the weird shit that had happened. We all had a tacit understanding that she wasn't to be fucked with, which isn't something you'd expect from four dudes. Camilla stood at five-feet-nothing, but I'd seen her make the biggest of men shrink away from her like wounded animals. She carried with her a kind of imposing darkness that could make the strongest men wilt at her will.

Watching Hank stand up to her was simultaneously awe-inspiring and terrifying. I feared for him in the moment. Either Johnny would kick him out of the band or she'd tear his throat out with her teeth.

Neither happened, of course, which made the argument even weirder.

"Day in, day out, we get to watch you parade yourself around this fucking studio like you own the place, like you own us. Leechin' off us. All because you've got this spineless coward by the balls." He gestured to Johnny, whose cheeks blossomed dark red with heat, fury. "What, you think because you're sitting on his dick every night—"

Camilla grinned. "Yours too, honey."

"—that you can come in here and dictate what goes on in this band? News flash, cunt: You ain't part of this band. You never were. You never will be. You're just a groupie, and it's all you ever will be. And *you*—" He wheeled around and opened his mouth to spew vitriol at Johnny, but our frontman had heard quite enough. Johnny's fist was waiting for him when Hank turned.

And…well, you get the idea. Blows were traded. By the time I managed to pull Bobby out of the studio and get him cleaned up, Hank and Johnny were collapsed at opposite ends of the studio. Their hair was disheveled, their shirts torn, their cheeks bruised and lips bloodied.

Camilla sat between them with her eyes closed, in the center of Johnny's makeshift Metatron design, with her legs crossed and back straight. She inhaled slowly and exhaled in a singular hum, filling the room, filling our heads, with a warm, even buzzing sound. All around us, candles perched on our equipment flickered and danced, casting erratic shapes along the walls.

When the humming stopped she opened her eyes and looked up at us. Her eyes glowed gold, and when she smiled at me I felt my balls shrivel up and hide. For the first time since we entered the room, I noticed she wasn't sitting on the floor. She was floating.

"I do hate when my subjects quarrel."

Camilla rose into the air and unfolded her legs. The

tips of her toes lightly brushed against the studio carpet. She floated toward us, brushed past me, and took Bobby's chin in her hand.

"Just five more minutes, Bobby. You can do that, can't you, hon?"

Bobby's teeth chattered. He tried to speak but couldn't, and nodded instead.

"Good boy," she said, kissing him on the cheek. She turned and let her feet touch the floor. "Back to it then, my Yellow Kings."

I made a call to Reggie that night when I got back to my room. He didn't answer, so I left him a message and asked him to call me back. When he did, I'd have a hell of a story for him. I'd had enough of the bullshit, of feeling like a hostage in my own band. Something had to give, and it was going to be me.

My frustration, anger, and resentment weren't enough to fill the pit of fear that had opened in my gut. I didn't know what Camilla was or where she came from, but what I'd experienced in the last few weeks left me fucking terrified. Whenever I closed my eyes, I saw those figures in red robes standing at the gates of the golden city. I saw them—*and they could see me.*

That night, for the first time since I was a child, I slept with the lights on.

I still do.

TRACK #6
BENEATH BLACK STARS

If I could see your face
Beneath these black stars
Burning —
I would tear out my
Eyes —
To keep from that awful
Yearning —

 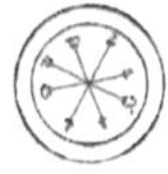  

Reggie called me back the following morning and told me to meet him at a small diner a couple blocks away. "Bring the guys," he said, "and let's talk about this." I told him I would, but I didn't say which guys. I roused Hank and Bobby from their rooms, but none of us bothered calling Johnny. He'd been staying at Camilla's loft, an invitation which had been extended to all of us, but none of us were brave enough to accept it. Hank and Bobby had had various trysts with her since that night in the hotel, but like I said before, I'd made it a point to stay as far away from her as possible. Besides, Johnny wasn't invited to this meeting.

Our manager was waiting for us in a booth at the far end of the diner. Three mugs of coffee were already on the table.

"Thought you might need this," he said, moving over. "Drink up. It's fresh."

We took our seats and nursed our coffee. Reggie was silent for a few minutes, watching each of us, inspecting us. Afterward, I realized he was looking for the signs he'd seen all too often in the business: track marks, scabs, bloodshot eyes, raw nostrils from too much coke. We had the bloodshot eyes covered—none of us had been sleeping well, something I think I already told you—but we were free and clear otherwise.

Still, old Reggie didn't mince words. "You boys look like dogshit."

None of us disagreed with him.

"So…you swear to me none of you have been using? Don't lie to me, guys."

We shook our heads, but Bobby and Hank looked to me to speak for the group. "No," I said. "You know us better than that. The only thing we do is drink, and we've kept ourselves sober for the recording. We wanted to stay sharp."

Reggie nodded. "Good, good. This Camilla, she's still clinging to Johnny?"

"That's one way of putting it," I said.

"Okay, then. Put it another way."

We took turns telling him what had transpired since we last saw him at the hotel all those weeks ago, down to the weird hallucinations which, to my surprise, had been happening to everyone. Bobby's fainting incident the night before was part of it.

"That's what happened to me," Bobby said. "I blacked out, but I was still awake, you know? And there was this weird city, with these weird people in robes, telling me to take off my mask or something. I stood up from my kit and meant to walk down to the shore, and…and that's where I blacked out for real, I guess. Next thing I remember is you guys crowded around me and Hank yelling at Johnny."

Hank recounted what happened after I took Bobby out of the studio to get cleaned up.

"So me 'n Johnny were going at it, right? Fucker can throw a good punch, I'll give 'em that. Anyway, I took a charge at him like a linebacker, and the next thing I know, I'm flying through the fuckin' air like goddamn Tinkerbell. Johnny, too. Camilla had stepped between us, but she never touched us. Not once. Whatever she did sent us flying at opposite ends of the room. When you guys came back into the studio, we weren't cowering from each other; we were cowering from *her*. And then she did that weird floating meditation shit."

Reggie perked up, his eyes as big as quarters. "Floating meditation shit?"

"Yeah," I said. "Kind of like that night in the hotel. Remember?"

Our old manager's cheeks blossomed a dark shade of maroon. He looked down at his cup of coffee and idly stirred the black brew with his spoon. The metal scraping against the ceramic mug gave me chills.

"I'd… I'd hoped that was just a bad dream."

Hank shook his head. "Wasn't a dream, Reg. We were all there. Those things she made us do…"

"I know," he whispered. He let go of his coffee mug and ran his fingers across the rim of his gold wedding band. "Honestly, I think I'd rather go back to believing it was a dream."

"So would we," I said. "We didn't mean to dredge up the past. Believe me, we'd rather leave it all behind us, but the point is, she's a problem. A real fucking problem."

Bobby piped up. "I don't feel safe, Reg. Like what we're doing in the studio feels wrong somehow. The candles, the incense, the weird positioning, all the hallucinations, it's like we're doing something unnatural. Like the music we're making isn't supposed to exist or something."

I thought about cutting in to say I didn't think they were hallucinations at all, but held my tongue. How might they react to something like that? And what good would it do? I felt foolish for even thinking such things, but the fear of that golden city mingled at the back of my mind. Whatever that place was, wherever it was, it sure as hell felt real to me. I could still feel the warm breeze blowing in from the sea, could smell the briny waves and hear them crash against the shore.

I could still hear the hushed whispers crawling over the dunes toward me.

"Take off your mask," I whispered. The others fell

silent and looked at me. "That's what they said. The figures in the robes."

"What do you think that means?" Reggie asked.

"No idea." I sighed. "And if it's all the same, I'd rather not know."

"Can't say I blame you, son." He sighed and sat back in his seat. "So what do we do?"

"What can we do?" Hank asked. "She's got him wrapped around her fucking finger. And we can't kick him out of the band. He's our lyricist."

Bobby shook his head. "We're not kicking him out. Johnny's the heart of the band. If it weren't for him, none of us would be here right now."

I considered our options. Camilla had managed to entwine herself around Johnny's heart. Like the others, I feared that if we cut her out, she'd take the best part with her—or worse, she'd kill him altogether, either in body or spirit. Or both.

I didn't like the idea of kicking Johnny out of the band. I also didn't like the idea of keeping Camilla around. Ultimately, I took the coward's way out, choosing to put off the decision at a later date. I still kick myself for it.

"Look," I said, "let's just finish the record. We can solve the Camilla problem when we're done. We can cross that bridge when we come to it. Deal?"

None of them had a better suggestion. Our silence sealed the agreement.

"I hate to be a killjoy," Reggie quipped, "but what if you're already on that bridge?"

We didn't have a clever answer to that question. Instead, we ate our breakfast in silence, and Reggie's words hung over us like a dense fog after a storm.

We took Reggie back to the studio after breakfast. Even though our conversation about what to do about Johnny and Camilla weighed heavily on all of us, we were still excited for him to hear the new material. I'll go on record and say that I'm proud of the music we made. From a technical standpoint, I don't think we ever played better than what we put down in that studio during those sessions. Even if things hadn't gone the way they did, if the album saw the light of day and our careers took off, we never would've risen above that record. *The Final Reconciliation* was our peak, and I think we would've spent the rest of our lives trying to top it.

The thought of those songs never getting a proper release does pain me at times. We poured everything we had into those recordings. If only they hadn't been tainted by Camilla's dark presence. If only…

The three of us sank into the sofa at the back of the control room and watched Reggie's reaction to our work, one song at a time. Joe had put together a rough mix of each song. Johnny's vocals were missing from a lot of them, but we had enough to give Reggie an idea of what we were doing.

And I have to tell you, Mr. Hargrove, his reaction was priceless. There's nothing in this world more satisfying than earning the respect of someone you admire.

The track list for the album was pretty much done. Johnny already had it all mapped out, one song segueing into the next. Reggie kicked back in the office chair and crossed his arms as the opening acoustic notes of 'Reconciliatory Matters' spilled out of the stereo speakers. Halfway through the introduction, he turned to us with a peculiar smile on his face.

"Is this an instrumental?"

Bobby shook his head. "Johnny hasn't decided yet. He was thinking about writing a few lines for it."

Reggie nodded. "Tell him not to bother. It's perfect as-is."

The track ended, kicking into the grimy crunch of 'Wanderer'. The opening was so abrupt it gave Reggie a start. He fidgeted in his seat and tapped his fingers to Bobby's machine gun percussion. That song was one of the few which contained Johnny's recorded vocals, and it had a hell of a hook in the chorus:

"Tell me, sweet lady / Under whose black stars do you lie? / Where are we going? / What have you done? / A handful of dust to blot out the sun / His kingdom of gold to defy."

By the time the second chorus came around, Reggie was already mouthing the words, drumming his fingers on the edge of the mixing board, and tapping his feet to the rhythm. He caught my stare and smiled. I can't properly tell you how proud that made me feel.

I'm not sure when the change happened. Probably around track three or four, maybe—either 'Dim Carcosa' or 'Usurper', I don't recall for sure. My memory becomes fuzzy after Reggie's smile. I remember the room around us vibrating, pulsing almost, as though the air itself was a curtain behind which a child was rapping their knuckles. The music grew distant, nowhere near as overpowering as it had been, a faint melody carried across the waves.

Because there *were* waves, crashing against the edge of a bluff upon which the studio sat. I blinked and looked around at my friends, who were each lost in some form of dream state, rocking gently to the breeze, the tide, the ghostly melody lilting from afar. We were again on the dunes outside Carcosa, beneath a fiery red sky upon which hung carrion black stars that twinkled and cast crawling shadows over us.

Disoriented and confused, I rose from my seat and took a couple of steps across the sand, peering down the beach where a masked congregation waited at the city gates, their ruby robes flapping carelessly in the breeze.

My every instinct told me to turn away and run, to flee from that impossible city, and I remember even feeling the twitch of my muscles spasm in agreement, but I didn't. Instead, I wandered across those darkened shores toward the congregation, and as I drew near, I discovered their robes were emblazoned with a golden symbol. The symbol was familiar to me, though I couldn't recall where I'd seen it.

One of the congregation, an unfathomably lanky creature draped in robes, heard my shaken voice and turned back to face me. I was taken aback by the mask it wore, a sickly white thing that bore the appearance of an androgynous human, the eyes black and lifeless, the mouth expressionless—and a series of gray nubs that squirmed and writhed just beyond the edge.

The robed creature approached. I stood motionless upon the sand, rooted in place by a fear I had never known before, and a cautious curiosity. What were these things? And was this really happening? If I turned back, would I find myself fast asleep in the control room? Part of me wanted to look back, to turn away from this gargantuan beast and the writhing things that moved behind its mask, but my curiosity got the better of me.

An oily, guttural voice rose from behind the creature's mask, choking out the words, "*Do you know the Yellow Sign?*"

In that moment I realized where I'd seen the symbol. The statue in Camilla's apartment, with its fingers poised and frozen at the point of mutilation. Hastur. The true Yellow King.

"I do," I whispered, my voice barely present, the sound of sandpaper grit against stone. "Will you take off your mask?"

"*As you wish,*" it said, raising a slender claw to its face. The red-robed thing pulled off its mask with a sickening wet sound. What I saw lurking, slithering, *nesting* in the vacuous hole of its face sent my mind spiraling into a maddened panic. The scream worked its way up my throat and across my quivering tongue, infecting the billowing fabric of reality, and alerting the other members of that blasphemous congregation.

I screamed until my insides were hot and raw, my vocal cords withering in a flame of my own kindling, and no matter how hard I tried, I could not take my eyes off the festering gray worms writhing and feeding within the thing's fleshy wound of a face.

The last thing I recall before Johnny woke me was the dry hiss of the congregation speaking as one: "*Coronate the usurper in the waters of Hali.*"

Moments later I was back in the control room, thrashing my arms and legs wildly against Johnny's restraint. A red haze clouded my vision, and for a time I thought I'd jumped from one nightmare to the next. My senses returned to me slowly as though they were a series of switches flipped on in succession, and I realized that awful noise filling my ears was my own pained shrieks.

"Aidan! Christ, dude, get a hold of yourself."

I sucked in air and held my breath to steady my racing heart. I counted to twenty, exhaled, and blinked. My vision remained hazy and dark. "Why…why can't I see?"

Johnny placed a tissue in my hand. "Because your eyes are bleeding."

Later, after I'd cleaned the blood from my face, I learned I wasn't the only one to suffer an 'episode' like that. Reggie, Hank, and Bobby had all experienced similar things, only they weren't foolish enough to wander down the shore toward the city. That was my own stupidity.

We sat in the control room for what might have been

hours, each of us suffering from what I can only describe as the worst hangover imaginable. Withdrawals, maybe. Hank's hands wouldn't stop shaking, and I heard Bobby crying at one point. Reggie stared off into space, mumbling incoherently to himself.

Camilla wandered through the room with a knowing smile. Watching her traipse through filled me with a quiet rage. I wanted to rise from my seat, grab her by the shoulders, and shake her. "How dare you?" I wanted to scream. "How dare you mock us?"

She knew what we'd seen, where we'd been. Somehow this was her doing, even if it was our music that unlocked the gate into that other place. She may not have put the instruments in our hands or told us what notes to play, but—

My rage faltered. But what, exactly? The anger drained from me, leaving me weak and drenched in a film of sweat. Camilla had everything to do with this and nothing at all. She was Johnny's inspiration for the greatest thing we'd ever done, and a cancer that was slowly devouring us one day at a time. Looking at her from across the room, a word crawled up out of my memory of Carcosa's distant shoreline: *usurper*. That's what she was. A usurper, not of a throne, but of our lives, upheaving everything we knew and cared about, twisting this journey of ours into something straight out of her own sickly twisted fantasies.

Somehow she'd imposed her will upon us without lifting a finger. Just as she'd bent our will in the hotel room that night, or made her eyes change color, or levitated off the ground. Was it the weird esoteric shit back at her apartment? Was it all that dark ritual magic bullshit? Or was it something else?

That moment, Mr. Hargrove, was when I began to suspect she wasn't who she said she was. I know you're probably wondering why it never occurred to me before, but in all honesty, until that moment I didn't give it a second thought because she didn't matter to me. Not really. She was just a groupie. A nomad we'd met on the road who was into some really freaky, kinky shit.

I think we'd all underestimated her until that day in the recording studio. That day we glimpsed her true intentions, and however puzzling they were at the time, they were equally horrifying.

Me, Hank, Bobby, and especially Reggie, we all got it. I'm afraid I couldn't say the same about Johnny. He saw things a little differently.

"What the fuck were you guys doing, anyway?"

Hank raised his head and frowned. "What do you mean? We were giving Reggie a taste of what we've been working on."

Johnny shook his head. "That's not what I mean, dipshit. I mean what the fuck were you doing here without me? None of you told me you were meeting with Reggie today."

"You weren't invited." Bobby leaned forward in his seat and stared daggers at our frontman. Johnny took off his shades and brushed the hair out of his face.

"Not invited?" He looked at Reggie. "I'm still a part of this band. I'm still under contract. I'm still the motherfucker responsible for carrying your asses through this process. And I'm still entitled to a percentage. Why the *fuck* was I not invited to this meeting?"

He'd balled his hands into fists, clenching them so tight that this arms shook. His cheeks darkened with a shade of bruise. I thought he was going to have a heart attack.

"*Carrying* our asses?" Hank shot to his feet. "Fuck that noise. We aren't the ones letting Yoko here make our decisions for us."

Finally, Reggie had heard enough. He climbed to his feet—shakily, I might add—and stepped between them.

"Johnny, for God's sake, calm down. It wasn't like that at all." Reggie put a hand on Hank's shoulder and shooed him back to his seat. "Aidan called and asked to meet up for breakfast. It was early, you were with your lady, and we didn't want to interrupt your quality time together. That's all. No big deal."

Johnny shot a glance at me. "Oh really?"

"Yeah," I said, "really. Just breakfast, Johnny. We got to talking about the recording and Reggie asked to come back here for a listen."

"Right," Reggie said, "and I love what I've heard so far."

"Isn't that lovely?" For the first time since we'd been roused from our hallucination, Camilla insinuated herself into the conversation. She stepped away from her corner of the room and cleared her throat. "I think you're lying, Reggie."

Our manager's face flushed red. "Lying? You can believe whatever you want to believe, lady. I don't have to prove shit to you."

"You don't have to, Reg. I can smell it on you like bad cologne. And you *are* wearing very bad cologne. It's called *Eau de Fear*." Camilla leaned in close to his chin and inhaled deeply through her nose. "It suits you."

Reggie opened his mouth to speak but stopped. He looked at me, then Johnny, then Hank and Bobby. Then he turned back to her and smirked. "Do you mind if we speak in private?"

Camilla's eyes lit up. They were different colors that day. Blue and green. She grinned and said, "Sure, Reggie."

The four of us watched him follow her out of the control room. Just before the door swung shut, I heard Reggie speak in his Scary Business Guy voice. I'd only ever heard him use that voice a couple of times before when we were on tour. It was a loud, deep, commanding voice that he used to straighten out uncooperative venue promoters.

"Let me explain to you how this is going to work, Camilla…"

The door swung shut. We didn't see what happened afterward, but we heard it. Camilla didn't like his explanation very much.

There were two sides to the story of what happened after that door closed.

According to Camilla, Reggie shoved her against the wall and slapped her so hard that her nose bled. She said he told her that if she didn't leave town, he'd call some of his friends down in the valley. Friends who were connected, if she got his drift. Friends who'd hold her down and let him have his way with her again just like that night in the hotel. Friends who wouldn't think twice about putting a bullet in her pretty little head. Friends who knew the best places to hide a body, places where no one would think to look for a no-name star-fucking whore like her.

Later, after we'd bailed him out of jail, Reggie told us that wasn't true at all.

"Well," he admitted, "except for calling her a no-name star-fucking whore. That part's true."

What really happened was, after the door closed, Reggie told her that she needed to back off and let us finish our job. "I told her I was sure she had a family somewhere that missed her terribly. I even offered her fucking bus fare to wherever she needed to go. She told me she lived here in LA—or Carcosa, as she called it—and I said, 'Whatever. Go home, then. You aren't welcome here.' And that's when she started hurting herself."

To hear Reggie tell it, Camilla flung herself back against the hallway wall, spun around, and cracked her face into the white cinderblock. He said she hit herself so hard he could hear the pop of her nose against the brick. I'll never forget that. The thought that a nose could simply go 'pop', like a burst balloon.

"She stood there for a moment, and when she turned around her eyes weren't different colors anymore. They were gold. Blood was gushing out of her nose, over her lips, staining her teeth as she smiled at me. And then she fucking *winked*, guys. She winked. And that's when the screaming started."

We heard her screams, and Johnny bolted out of the room to her aid. He found her exactly as she wanted him to, crumpled on the floor, sobbing incoherently as blood streamed down her face. Reggie was standing there, frozen in shock, all color drained from his cheeks.

And the rest, well, you can imagine how it went. Johnny freaked out, called the cops, screamed that he wasn't just going to fire Reggie, but press charges and sue his ass into oblivion.

Had we not been so close to wrapping up the album, I think we would've called it quits there. But even after all the drama, after Reggie left us for the day to go meet with his attorney, we still went back to that goddamn studio to finish our music.

All we had left were some vocal tracks to put down. Johnny went into the booth, leaving the rest of us to listen in the control room. And Camilla, too, who sat on the floor in her corner, blood drying on her upper lip and chin, giggling quietly to herself.

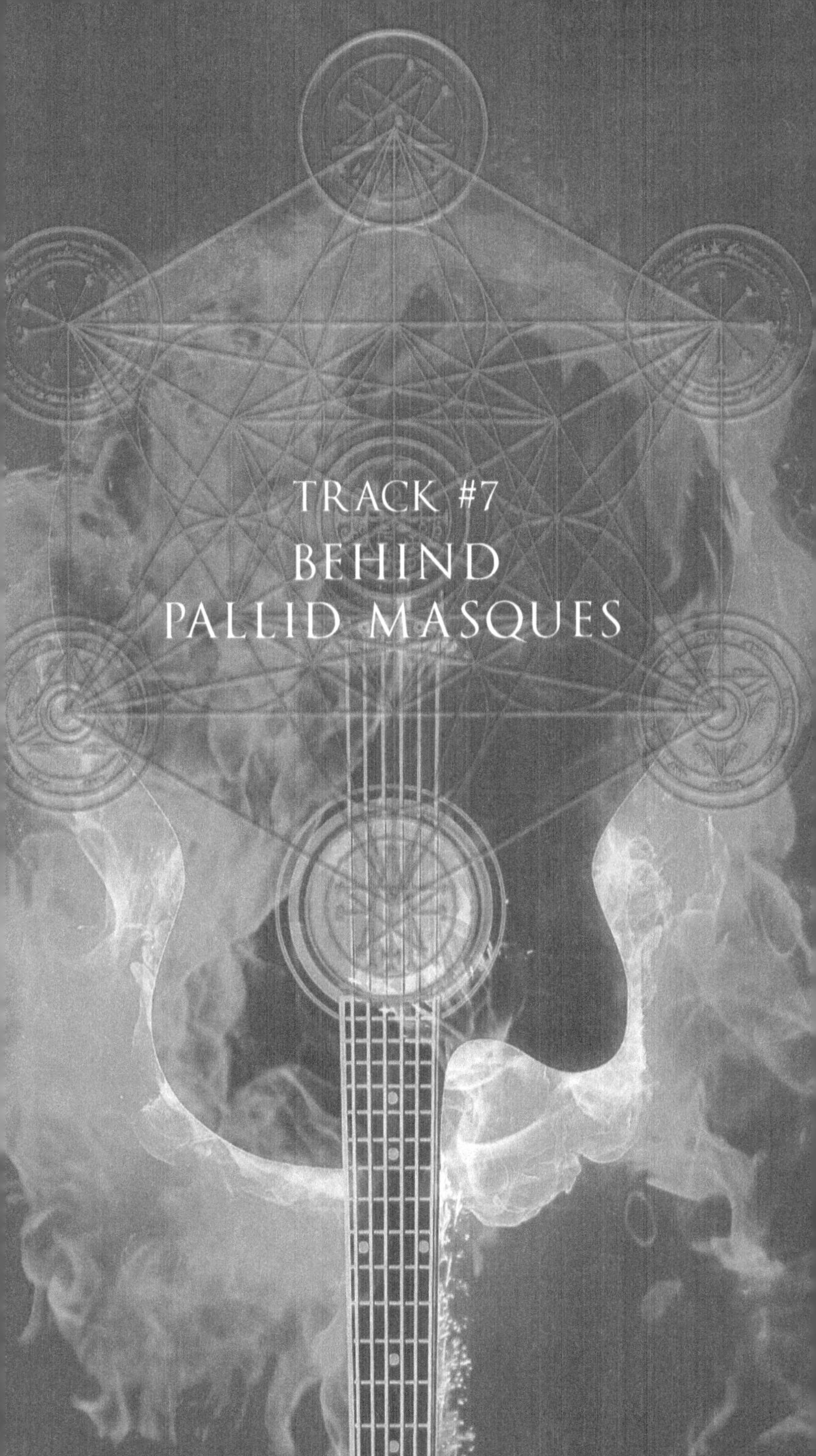

TRACK #7
BEHIND
PALLID MASQUES

You cast me out

To these lands of the damned

I will rip off all their masques

And hold their faces

in my hands

 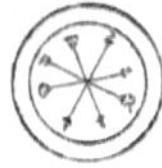  

Camilla dropped the charges on the condition that Reggie keep his distance from her. In truth, it was her way of keeping him away from Johnny and the rest of us. Reggie was a wildcard in the scheme of things, the only real opposing force that could present any threat to whatever she was up to. That much is obvious to me now, but back then, we were so tired and scared and drunk on the hope of wrapping up the album that we didn't give it much thought. We were just sick of the drama and wanted to be done with it.

I can understand why some bands implode, and I can understand why some take years between records. You work with the same people long enough, they become family, but that doesn't mean you don't get tired of seeing them day in and day out. Sometimes you just get sick of their shit. Sometimes you need a break to recharge, and sometimes that takes years to do.

We wrapped up recording the album with Joe a few days after the incident with Reggie. Me, Hank, and Bobby had agreed to take some time off after we were finished. Time to think about our future, whether we wanted to continue with the band or call it quits after the album's release. I remember having a long talk with Bobby one night at the hotel, about whether or not we'd be willing to walk away and leave everything to Johnny. We'd continue earning royalties for the record sales, but Johnny had rights to the band name, and he'd be free to record future albums under the moniker.

And you know, we were fine with that. After that last month of hell, and after we understood that Camilla wasn't going away, we were fine with walking away from it all. Let Johnny continue his slow descent into madness. Let Camilla suck out whatever soul was left inside that dried-up husk of his body.

We finished the album, but we never got that break. Camilla had other plans.

Two things happened the morning I'd planned to fly back home. The first was a call from Johnny, wanting to know how I felt about playing a secret show there in LA to build hype for the album. The second: I made a decision to leave the band.

I remember that morning clearly. I was awake before dawn, pulled from sleep by nightmares of the dark shoreline outside the golden city. Those faceless things in red robes were there, asking me about yellow signs, and finally—mercifully—I'd awakened in a cold sweat. I couldn't get back to sleep, nor did I want to. I rose from bed and looked out the window at the city in those pre-dawn hours. I remember thinking everything looked so insignificant, miniscule. Out there was a world of people with problems of their own, and not a single one of them mattered. The people or their problems. This depressed me something awful, and I stepped away to clean myself up.

After I showered, I stood in front of the bathroom mirror and stared at my face, noting the lines and circles around my eyes. I'd lost weight, at least twenty pounds, and my eyes were swollen and bloodshot from sleep loss. When I stepped back, I could count my ribs. Growing up, I was a scrawny kid, but I filled out when I reached my twenties. Looking at myself that morning, I was startled to see that I'd regressed into a withered state. My body looked haggard, aged, like driftwood washed up on the shore.

I thought about something Camilla said that night in the van. God, it felt like such a long time ago, when in reality it had only been something like a month? Six weeks? Doesn't matter. She'd said, "I want to help you take off your mask."

My whole face looked like a mask. Like I was wearing someone else's face, like the person I used to be was still underneath there somewhere.

And then I remembered my hallucination. The voice drifting across the sand. *Take off your mask.* At the time I hadn't yet decided if what I'd experienced during my hallucinatory episodes was real or not. I wasn't questioning if there was something waiting beyond the fabric of time and space. Carcosa was just a dream to me. A nightmare, something introduced to me by Johnny's Yellow Queen.

I traced my fingertip across my forehead—like this—and then around my face. For one real agonizing moment, I actually thought about tearing into my flesh to see what was hiding underneath. I was possessed with the notion that I was still in there somewhere, and the only reason I didn't do it is because I remembered what those red-robed things looked like underneath their masks. I was terrified that I wouldn't be me underneath my face. Afraid all that lurked beneath this façade of humanity was a dark gaping hole filled with bulbous, gray coffin worms, writhing and feasting on the rot.

When I snapped out of the trance, I saw I'd cut myself along my temple. A tributary of blood had formed along the ridge of my jawline, seeping into the edge of my beard. The sight of my own blood startled me and was enough to help me make the decision to leave.

For as great as it was, the band and the music we made together wasn't worth the cost of my sanity.

I'd resolved to call a meeting with the band when my phone rang. Johnny was on the other end.

"Aidan," he said, "listen, I have an idea…"

Two hours later I was sitting in the lobby. Hank and Bobby were with me, each of us nursing a steaming cup of horrible hotel coffee. Johnny and Camilla were late.

We sat in silence. We'd done that a lot lately. None of us wanted to discuss the things we had to talk about, none more so than me. I chose to keep my decision silent until Johnny arrived and explained his plan in detail. I'll be the first to admit I didn't want to break the news to any of them; I'd also be lying if I said I wasn't interested in hearing more about this show. Either way, I was teetering between divorcing myself from the band and going out on another tour to 'get away from it all'.

I replayed the phone conversation in my head: "I have an idea," Johnny had said. "I was thinking about how we're going to present this music to our fans, and you know how a lot of these bands are going on nostalgia tours, playing whole albums live? What if we did that before the album drops? We can keep it a secret, make it a big mysterious thing for the fans. Camilla knows a promoter at a club downtown…"

And that's when I'd tuned out. It wasn't really a conversation at all. Johnny had always bounced his ideas off me, but when he mentioned her name, I knew in my heart that this wasn't his idea at all. It was hers. Johnny hated marketing anything. When we went on tour for the *Jesters in Our Court* EP, he didn't even want to deal with having a merch booth. Marketing was someone else's job, he reasoned. Besides, it took time away from his 'art'.

Hearing him talk about hype and fans just felt wrong somehow. I thought back to my earlier moments staring into the mirror, wondering if I was still me underneath my mask, and shivered. What had she done to him? What had she done to us all? And why?

Ah, yes. "Why?" Never underestimate man's desire for closure. Even now, I question if my need to understand was driven out of some sick sense of duty to the band, or if it was to satisfy my own fearful curiosity. Part of me wanted to know that all the hell we'd suffered in the last several weeks had been for something; the other part just wanted to grasp her intentions. Intentions that, like the coveted brass ring, were always just a few inches beyond our reach of understanding.

If I was going to walk away from my career over this, I needed to know why. I'd made up my mind to confront her, to try and get some answers out of her. I just had to get her alone, without her watchdog there to get in my face.

I was in the middle of working out just how to go about doing that when Johnny and Camilla strolled through the hotel lobby. I almost didn't recognize him. Johnny's long hair was dirty, and his shirt—a faded Opeth tee—had several holes along the lower hemline. He looked like what I imagine Layne Staley did in his final days before his heroin overdose.

Camilla, however, looked incredible. Like a model, maybe, or a really well-paid escort. Her auburn hair shone in the morning light, drawing out the color of her eyes, which were hazel and brown, just like the night we first met. The contrast between the two of them was startling. *Christ*, I thought, *she's sucking the life from him.*

"Good morning, fellas." He stopped before us. "Want to go get some breakfast?"

Hank and Bobby mumbled in agreement. I hadn't given much thought to food until he said something, and my stomach growled in reply.

"Great," Camilla said. She winked at me. "I know a place a few blocks away."

The diner was crowded, and we had to wait twenty minutes for a table. We made idle chit-chat in the meantime, nothing worth noting, and twice Johnny asked me if there was something wrong. I had a hard time looking him in the eye. Not just because I'd made up my mind about leaving—that was part of it—but also because he just looked ill. Older. Withered. What had become of my friend? Had I witnessed this happening every day and just not noticed? Or was this something that had occurred overnight?

For the first time in weeks I thought of Johnny's mother, sitting in her room at the hospital, staring off into nothingness. She hadn't been present in her own mind for years, and I couldn't help but wonder if this is how it had begun for her. Perhaps this was how she'd begun her descent into madness, aging overnight, obsessing over a work of art that wasn't meant for this earth. Maybe Johnny was just following in her footsteps.

No. I shook that thought away from my mind. Johnny was fine until Camilla latched onto him. I could've told her to fuck off that night in Texas. I could've kicked her to the curb as just another meaningless groupie.

But I didn't, and I felt horrible for that. I felt responsible somehow, like I'd let him down by not protecting him from this horrible woman.

After we were seated and had ordered our meals, Johnny got down to business.

"So, like I said on the phone, I was thinking we could do a secret show. I know you guys are worn out from the studio and everything that happened, but me and Camilla have been talking—"

Hank rolled his eyes. "Shocking."

"—and we think it would be good for the band if we put on a show to stretch our legs."

We think. Meaning Johnny and Camilla. *We.* Not me, Hank, or Bobby. If I hadn't been sandwiched between Hank and Bobby in our booth, I think I would've walked out of that little meeting.

"Since Reggie's out of the picture, we have to start thinking about ourselves as a business."

I cleared my throat and spoke up. "But Reggie isn't out of the picture, Johnny."

"Oh, yes he is," Camilla said. She pointed to her nose. "I don't want him anywhere near me."

Johnny nodded. "Agreed. I want to replace him as soon as possible."

"You didn't let me finish," I said. "He's under contract, too, Johnny. The only way he goes out of the picture is if we take him to court. Do you want to do that? Do *any* of you want to do that?" I gave the table some room to breathe. No one said anything. "This is Reggie, guys. He got us this far. Kicking him to the curb is wrong. I don't care what she says he did. None of us saw it happen. It's her word against his." I met her stare and frowned. If we'd been alone, I think she would've clawed my eyes out based on the way she was glaring at me. "In that sort of argument, he's going to win every time. I do *not* trust her."

Hank and Bobby nodded in agreement. Johnny leaned back and sighed.

"Guys," he said, "all right, let's discuss Reggie later. Can we get back to planning the show?"

"Planning?" Hank scoffed. "We ain't even agreed to it."

"Okay, yeah, you're right. Just hear me out. Can you give me that much, at least?"

Johnny's proposition was simple: we book a venue, invite some friends and journalists, and play the album live. The whole thing in its entirety. Nine Inch Nails did it during their first 'farewell' tour, joining the likes of Rush, Pink Floyd, A Perfect Circle, and a handful of others. "The difference," Johnny said, "is they won't be expecting it. They'll be expecting a few new songs mixed with the ones from the EP."

"Think about it," Camilla said. "You get a couple hundred rock journalists at your show, and play them new material that won't be available until next year. The hype alone will sell a million records. You'll go platinum in no time."

"Excuse me," Bobby said, "but when did you become a record executive?"

Camilla only smiled at him, but the look in her eyes screamed murder. Johnny cut in: "She's just trying to help, guys. I don't understand why you have all this animosity toward her."

"You don't understand?" I looked at the guys, who appeared just as incredulous as I was. Was Johnny so blind that he didn't see what was happening? "Don't you remember the night in the hotel? Or the weird shit that went down in the studio? Have you looked at yourself in a mirror lately?"

Johnny's mouth hung agape as he turned his gaze from me, to Hank, to Bobby, and back to Camilla. He smiled and chuckled to himself. "No, I don't know what you're talking about."

"I'm being serious, Johnny."

He took off his glasses and slammed his fist on the table. "So am I. I'm not looking to start a fight with you, Aidan, but goddammit, I'll finish one if I have to."

I honestly didn't know what to say. I'll admit I started to question my own sanity right then. Perhaps all of this shit was just in my head. Maybe everything we'd seen hadn't happened that way after all. Never mind that Hank and Bobby had confirmed everything during our meeting with Reggie a few days earlier.

Camilla put her hand on Johnny's. "Shhh, it's okay. Calm down, love." She drummed her fingers on the table. "Just one show, guys. Give me one show to organize for you. If it doesn't work out the way you want it to, I'll stay out of your business."

Hank smirked. "And let's say it does work out. What then?"

"Then you won't have to look for a new manager while you wait out Reggie's contract."

Bobby and Hank looked at me, and I looked to Johnny. He smiled and took Camilla's hand.

"My Yellow Kings," she cooed. "My boys. I'll take you to places you've never been. I'll take you through Carcosa's gates."

The waitress brought our breakfast orders after that. Everyone else ate in silence; I only picked at my meal. Every time I looked at my pancakes, I thought of one of those red-robed things. I thought of holes. I thought of worms.

Carcosa's gates. The thought of what lay beyond them turned my stomach. With my appetite thoroughly ruined, I got up and excused myself from the table.

Okay, so I'm going to put all my cards on the table here, Mr. Hargrove. I admit that what Johnny and Camilla were proposing did sound really cool. At the time, I don't think anyone had played a full album live before it had even dropped in stores. We didn't have to worry about bootleg recordings since every person on the guest list would be screened and checked at the door.

And to be honest, I couldn't wait to play the new material. Out of this whole affair, I think the loss of the music is one of our greatest tragedies. What the music did to us was terrible, but it was also the greatest work we ever produced. Just talking about it now makes my fingers itch, and I haven't touched a guitar in years. If my hands weren't so knotted with arthritis, I'd probably be strumming a few chords for you right now.

All of that said, when push came to shove, we agreed to do the show. I think all of us wanted an opportunity to do a 'live fire exercise' with the new material, and really see how it would resonate with people.

Camilla did have conditions, however. If we wanted to use the resources at her disposal (which were considerable for a so-called wanderer such as herself—one look at her lavish loft apartment told us as much), we had to agree to give her full autonomy over the set design. I remember thinking it all had something to do with Johnny's sacred geometry placement in the studio, which speaks more to my naivety than anything else.

We never did find out where her fortune came from. In the days leading up to the show, Hank made a joke about her lady parts being made of gold as an explanation for her apparent wealth. As crass at it was, I admit I chuckled the first couple of times he told it.

Beyond set design, Camilla made that show possible, which is the exact position she wanted to be in. She knew Reggie was our checkbook, and that the record label never would've agreed to fund such a live show. It's a wonder that Reggie didn't cut off our funds and have us booted from the hotel. I still don't know why he didn't. Probably out of fear of retaliation. Camilla had had him locked up once for assault and battery; he'd seen firsthand what sort of bullshit she could get away with.

Camilla had friends, too. The owner of the club we booked was a short, slimy guy by the name of Vinnie Klorso. You know the type. If she'd told us he owned a couple of used car lots, I wouldn't have been surprised. He kept his hair dyed jet black and greased back on the top. Bobby once told me he reminded him of his creepy uncle who always wanted a hug; I told him he reminded me of a shorter, slimier Mike Patton, without the talent or vocal range.

Vinnie owned a club down on the strip called The Hyades, after some ladies from Greek mythology. The place was tiny, one of those exclusive clubs that keep people waiting outside for hours, with a max occupancy of 250 including staff.

"The place is perfect," Camilla told us during our tour of the place. "Spatially and spiritually. Can't you feel the vibrations of the drapery here? They're perfectly frail. It's like you could just slip your hand right through them and touch the other side." She'd sucked in her breath and let her eyes roll back. "This place is perfect for transubstantiation."

A few weeks before, we would've rolled our eyes and said she was tripping out of her mind, but after the hallucinations we'd experienced in the studio, her words made us uneasy. There was a weight to them. Had we slipped beyond this 'drapery' before? I suspected we had, even if what we'd experienced had only felt like the worst kind of nightmare—the kind you wake up from clawing at your skin, terrified that what you saw is still with you, crawling across your body, suffocating you like a dark shroud.

"We can position candles here, here, and here."

Vinnie interjected. "I hope you mean fake candles, Camilla darling. Fire codes and all."

"Oh, don't worry, Vinnie dearest." She'd caught my eye and smirked. "Of course I mean the fake kind."

This probably goes without saying, especially since the fire chief's report has been public record for decades, but that was a bold-faced lie. She used real candles. Black ones.

"Vinnie, dear, will you have a problem with drapery hung at the back of the stage?"

"Not at all, Camilla darling."

We were at the club for hours as Camilla and Johnny mapped out their plan for the show. Every inch of the place would be decorated in red and gold: Gold drapery, gold sconces for the candles, red banners everywhere, you name it. A giant golden throne would sit at center stage, just in front of the elevated riser from which Bobby would be drumming. The club staff—bartenders, waiters and waitresses, security— were to be dressed in red robes and white masks. Every one of our guests that night would be given a white mask at the door and asked to wear it for the duration of the show.

When she told us that, a wave of nausea crashed over me. Was this really happening? Had my nightmares come true? Camilla's words raced back through my mind.

I'll take you through the gates of Carcosa.

I want to help you take off your mask.

Together we will sing the song of the Hyades in the court of Carcosa.

Cold hands gripped my insides and squeezed. The world swam before me, a maelstrom of red and gold, faces with holes and worms, all spinning down the bloodied drain of an impossible cyclopean city.

"Aidan?"

I blinked and steadied myself. Camilla, Vinnie, and the band were all staring at me.

"Y-Yeah?"

"You don't look so hot," Hank said. "You all right?"

"Just need some air," I said, nearly tripping over my own feet as I retreated across the open floor and back toward the exit. I made it as far as the sidewalk before I collapsed to my knees and vomited into the street. What little I'd eaten at breakfast left me in a runny, bilious blob, mingling with the trash in the gutter.

I don't know how long I knelt there on the sidewalk. The noonday sun beat down upon me, and heat shimmered above the pavement. I peered down the boulevard, watching traffic crawl along toward the city. Her city. Los Angeles, Carcosa, it didn't matter. This was her city now. Perhaps it had always been.

Somewhere in between the flickering folds of heat rising from the earth, I spied the tell-tale towers jutting just above the Hollywood Hills. They were thin cylindrical needles of unfeasible construction, sprouting to the air at bizarre angles. Crouched on the sidewalk, with spittle dribbling down my chin, I swear I could hear the hum of a thousand voices speaking in unison. Each syllable crawled across the hills, down across the paved hell of the Sunset Strip, and up into my ears, whispering words I never wanted to hear again: *Take off your mask, Aidan. Take off your mask.*

"I brought you some water."

Camilla stuck a bottle of water in my face. I took it from her reluctantly, examining the seal around the cap before taking that first drink. Satisfied that it hadn't been tampered with, I took two deep gulps before having to catch my breath. Water dripped down through my beard and pooled on the sidewalk below me.

"Thanks," I gasped. I took two more drinks before the feverish nausea finally subsided. In that time, Camilla took a seat beside me. Her auburn hair radiated in the sunlight, and I noticed her eyes were different colors. Green and blue.

"The nausea will pass," she said. "Carcosa has that effect once it gets into your head. But you'll be fine soon enough."

"How do you do that?"

"Do what?" she asked.

"The thing with your eyes. Contacts?"

Camilla leaned her head back and laughed. She never did answer that question, and to this day I have no idea what was up with the color of her eyes.

"Right," I said, feeling foolish for even asking. I held up the bottle of water. "Is this supposed to be a peace offering?"

"No. It's supposed to help you clear your head. So you can make up your mind."

"Make up my mind?"

She placed her hand on my knee and squeezed lightly. "I know you want to leave the band. Don't worry, Johnny doesn't know. I haven't told him, and I won't."

I didn't even bother asking how she knew. By this point it seemed natural that she would know such things, and I wasn't at all surprised.

"And you *can* leave," she went on. "I won't stop you. All I ask is that you play this final show."

"What is it about this show? What is it about Johnny? Why him? Or us, for that matter?"

I expected her to laugh me off again, but to my surprise, she didn't. Instead, I got an answer that chills me to my core every time I think about it.

"Because you are my way into Carcosa. I was cast out long ago, and with your help, you will secure my return. And the key, my dear Aidan, is here behind your mask. Behind all your masks. This world is nothing more than a masquerade, and your music will help us all to remove the masks that obscure the truth of Carcosa's golden light. A final reconciliation of this world and ours. Feel honored, my darling Yellow King. You will be home soon enough."

And with that, she climbed to her feet and patted me on the head like the dimwitted child I was.

"Carcosa is calling, Aidan. I hope you're ready. What you've seen thus far is only a glimpse of its glory. I can't wait to show you the rest."

I wasn't ready then. I'm not now, and I never will be. There's a cold fear buried deep within me that what I've seen is what awaits me after my life is over. That's what I fear most about my impending mortality, Miles. In my worst nightmares, I'm one of those things worshiping at the golden altar of Carcosa. Worshiping not a king known as Hastur, but a queen who calls herself Camilla.

I'm terrified that when I pass off this mortal plane, I'll find myself lost on those darkened shores, clad in robes and wearing a pallid mask that hides the cowardly truth of my essence: A stark emptiness, bottomless and rotted, fed upon by hundreds of crawling worms.

TRACK #8
THE
FINAL RECONCILIATION

Your Resistance to Truth
is Vile
I Don't Need Your Repudiation
You Can Suffer in Torment
While We Call For The
Final Reconciliation
Under Twin Moons I Give
My Life
I Will Untie The Binding-Lines
I Pray This Blood Will
Suffice
To Honor His Yellow Sign
Take Off Your Mask!

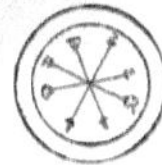

We were four days into rehearsals when Bobby asked the question. "What the hell does all this even mean?"

"Which part?" Johnny asked. He was in the middle of adjusting the microphone stand. One of the hired roadies had underestimated Johnny's height.

"This," Bobby said, gesturing around the stage. "The album. The art. All this gold shit. Half your lyrics are fucking riddles, dude."

Bobby had a point, although I'd been able to piece together just enough to follow a narrative running through each song. Johnny, however, took a cue from his girlfriend and played coy, merely shrugging with a smile.

"Haven't you been paying attention?" Johnny asked. "All will be revealed tonight." He tapped his microphone. "Check-check, one, two, three…"

Bobby looked at me and shrugged. Hank just shook his head.

"I stopped trying weeks ago, brother."

I would've walked them through the album, what I'd been able to piece together in my own head, but just kept my mouth shut. I was more curious about why we'd only been rehearsing a handful of the songs at a time, rather than playing through the full album in one session. We'd rehearsed the album in sections instead, playing three pieces at a time before taking a break. Then we'd start again from the top, only we'd experiment with different keys and arrangements. That was Hank's idea, believe it or not. He'd suggested it to keep the songs fresh while on tour.

Anyway, the fact that we were only rehearsing a handful of songs at a time seemed odd to me. I mean, I understand it now, but back in the days leading up to the show, it was just another one of the many riddles I couldn't unravel. Considering what had happened in the studio, the reason should have been no surprise to me, but….well, I'll get to that.

For that night's show, Johnny and Camilla had some theatrics planned as well—Vinnie was going to walk out and introduce us, Camilla's big statue of her Yellow King would be wheeled onstage, after which we'd take our places clad in red robes and white masks. That last part made me uneasy, but when I brought up the hallucinatory dream-space we'd all occupied in the studio, Johnny told me to shut the fuck up and relax.

Considering this would be my last time playing with the band, I figured I'd do as he told me for the sake of keeping the peace. Bobby and Hank were free to stay if they wanted, but I was done after this. What did it matter if I had to play dress-up?

Still, the idea did not sit well with me. When Camilla opened the cardboard box that contained the masks, I felt a hint of nausea stir in my gut. She saw me staring and smiled at me. "Don't worry," she said. "You will take these off before you begin the show. It's everyone else who has to wear them."

Like that was supposed to make me feel better.

The day of the show, we wasted no time in jumping into rehearsals. It was our last opportunity to do so, as we had a small interview scheduled with a reporter from one of the major metal review sites later that afternoon. We played a warm-up session with our songs from the *Jesters in Our Court* EP, opening this time with 'Holes in the Fabric'.

Once the blood was flowing, we jumped straight into the opening notes of 'Reconciliatory Matters'. Johnny did write lyrics for that one but begrudgingly agreed that Reggie was right, that it should remain an instrumental track.

We played up through the last movement of 'Dim Carcosa'. Johnny let his vocals fade out as he stepped away from the microphone, and I unplugged my guitar, but Hank and Bobby kept playing. Hank plucked the opening bass line to 'Usurper', which prompted Bobby to join in with his double kick drum.

The machine gun *ratta-tat-tat* of that song always got my heart pounding, and watching Hank and Bobby do their thing in tandem like that was a sight to behold. They fed off each other's energy, and the harder Bobby played, the faster Hank played to match him. I remember standing back in awe as they opened that song. Wait, that's not even the best way to describe it. They didn't open that song. They tore into it with a fucking axe, right into its heart. I wished I hadn't unplugged my guitar, or else I would've joined them, and I was about to do that very thing when I caught sight of a figure standing just off stage.

At first, I thought it was one of the guitar techs we'd hired to assist us with the show—they'd been working in tandem with us, tuning the equipment as needed—but the figure was much too tall. My blood froze once I realized what it was. Not who, mind you, but what. One of the things from my hallucination, clad in a crimson robe, with its face obscured behind a white mask.

My head swam, and the world took on a watery glaze, shimmering with a bizarre light. Was this really happening? Or had I lost myself in the music again? I could no longer tell. My bandmates made no mention of the robed thing lurking just off stage. They were too caught up in their jam, punishing their instruments with the notes we'd written together.

I lost sight of the creature when Johnny walked in front of me. One moment it was there, the next it wasn't. You're probably thinking it was all in my head, or that it was just a phantom of my imagination. You might be right, and you might be wrong about it. All I know is that I saw what I saw, and for the first time it wasn't in some dream-place of my own creation. It was there, ten feet away, standing off to the side of the stage.

Johnny shook his head and called out to the others. "No, no, cut it, guys. Come on."

Hank and Bobby did as he asked, but looked visibly deflated as they did so. For a full minute they'd been caught up in the fury and joy of the music we'd made together. Now Johnny was interrupting them, shouting for them to stop. And for why? None of us knew.

Hank caught my eye. He never said anything to me, and he didn't have to. He looked so defeated right then, like he was trapped and torn between leaving and continuing on without his artistic dignity. Had things not turned out the way they did, I think that would've been the end of Hank's tenure in the band as well. Hell, we probably would've flown home to Kentucky together. Maybe Bobby, too.

"Come on, Johnny," Hank sighed. "We were jamming, dude. Just let us play."

"And I ask you to just trust me on this." Johnny reached over and took a drink from his water bottle. "You don't want to burn yourself out before tonight."

Hank frowned. "Burn myself out? Christ, man, that's never going to happen if you don't let me play." He nodded to me and Bobby. "Let's go get lunch."

The three of us made our way off the stage, leaving Johnny alone with the instruments. Which was fitting, I think. He felt right at home there. It's where he'd spend the rest of his life.

After lunch, we went back to the hotel to relax for a few hours before sound check. I had a killer headache that I'd hoped to sleep off, popping a few aspirin shortly before falling face-first into bed. I'm not sure how long I lay there, watching the dark colors swirl and dance behind my eyes like a gothic kaleidoscope, but I do remember counting in time to the beating in my skull.

Sleep hadn't come easy to me in weeks. Catching a nap was something I'd not been able to do with any regularity since we'd started recording the album. There was simply too much to do, too much on my mind, or worse, too much waiting for me when I closed my eyes. That time, however, I remember I felt particularly safe inside my own head, and for as uncomfortable as it was, the 4/4 beat of my head helped lull me to sleep.

I should've known better. They were waiting for me to let my guard down.

Well, that's not quite true. I mean, I'm not *sure* if that's true or not. "Waiting" implies they had ill intent, and all these years later, I still don't know what their intent was.

The beating in my head ceased, and I opened my eyes. The muted, neutral cream-colored hotel walls were gone, displaced by the open air of Carcosa's dark shoreline. The briny stench from the hissing tides of Lake Hali wafted over my face, and black stars twinkled in a dusk-lit sky overhead. I sat up on the bed and watched in astonished horror as a pair of reddened moons rose upon the horizon, one eclipsing the other in an eternal cosmic dance. When I turned to follow them, I saw the red congregation marching along the shoreline toward the golden gates of the city.

A faint song floated along the air, filling my head with its melancholy tune. It wasn't one of our songs. That much was apparent. The somber tune lacked Johnny's edge and cadence, and the way the congregation hummed the notes gave it a funerary quality:

"*Songs that the Hyades shall sing / Where flap the tatters of the King / Must die unheard in / Dim Carcosa.*"

I rose from my bed, and against my better judgment, once again made my way down the dune toward the shore. I followed in the footsteps of beings greater than myself, pieces of a cosmic whole I could never fathom, could only speculate upon, serving as a constant reminder that my place in this universal tapestry was but a mere speck of paint. The world itself had taken on a shimmering impressionistic quality, the horizon watery with dim light of the twin moons, and the black stars dripped and bled like disturbed ink.

I followed the red congregation to the gates of Carcosa. There we paused, and their singing ceased. Together they turned toward me, an army of red and white and gold. The nearest creature approached and stopped before me. It reached out and beckoned to me, gesturing to my chest. I glanced down and discovered I wore an amulet of some crude design, a black onyx jewel carved with a golden sigil. Confused, I clasped the jewel in my hand and held it out before me as far as it would stretch. The robed creature nodded its head in understanding.

"*The yellow sign,*" it whispered. A thick, black substance seeped out from beneath the pallid mask like molasses, dribbling over the writhing nubs of worms and soaking into the crimson cowl around the creature's neck. "*A symbol of the King.*"

A sensation of vertigo overcame me, and I turned back to gaze upon my point of origin along the beach. The hotel bed was still there, the blankets wrinkled and disturbed by my exit, and the lamp stood upon the nightstand. The lampshade shuddered in the breeze.

I turned back to the creature and held up the onyx jewel. "Do you know the Yellow Sign?"

"*I do*," whispered the creature, as thick dollops of black ooze fell over the cuff of the robe and clumped at our feet. It raised one pale hand and unseated the mask from its viscous maw. I sucked in my breath, anticipating the impossible horror that I knew waited beneath that false face, and forced myself not to look away. Dozens of gray worms lazily searched the air like fingers jutting from the rim of that bottomless pit, an endless sinkhole of mystery into which no man could ever venture or know. We stared at one another for a beat, and I struggled to retain my wits. The putrid stench of rot and disease infected the air around us.

"*Will you unmask?*"

I touched my fingers to my face. "Should I?"

A low hiss of sickly wet air rose up out of the thing's empty face. "*Yes, the time to unmask is at hand.*" The creature reached out and brushed its long, pale fingers against my cheek. "*Take off your mask.*"

"But I'm—"

My eyes snapped open to the vibrating buzz of my phone. I sat up with a jolt, kicking my legs over the edge of the bed. The walls of my room were intact, and although the shoreline was gone, I could still smell the sweaty brine stench of…what was it? Not an ocean. A lake. But what was it called? No matter how much I searched my memory, I could not remember at the time. The dream-place of Carcosa had that effect.

The phone kept ringing. Annoyed, I picked it up and answered.

"Yeah?"

"Aidan? I didn't think you'd answer." Reggie's voice was shaky with relief. "I was starting to think you were ignoring my calls."

"No, no way, man. Sorry. I was catching a nap before our show."

"Yeah, I heard about that. A buddy of mine works for the Times and called to get the scoop. Had to tell him I didn't have one to give 'em, can you believe it? Me, without a scoop on my own band?"

My cheeks flushed with heat. "Reggie, I—"

"Don't sweat it, kid. I know it's not your doing. But I'm calling you about the show, just the same."

"What do you mean?"

"I mean I'm calling to ask you not to play the show."

His words hung in my head for a moment. "It's a little late for that, don't you think? We've been rehearsing for a week. Invitations went out two weeks ago. We—"

"Aidan, listen to me. Just—if you're going to play, play the old stuff. Don't play the new stuff."

There was fear in his voice, a kind of fear I'd not heard before. He sounded as though he were near tears. The more he spoke, the higher in pitch his voice grew.

I closed my eyes and sighed. "Reggie, the new stuff is the point. It's to build hype for the album. To take it for a test drive. You know how it is."

Camilla's words felt wrong on my tongue, but they came so easily, so naturally, that I felt guilty for uttering them. They were part of a language that Reggie would understand.

"Yeah, kid, I know that. But please, for God's sake, I'm begging you, don't play those songs tonight. I just got a bad feeling."

"You never struck me as the superstitious type, Reg."

"Always time to start bein' one, Aidan."

"Look, if it's any consolation, tonight's my last show. I'm done after this."

"I'm beg—wait, really?"

"You heard me." I looked at the cheap alarm clock

on the nightstand. I needed to get ready twenty minutes ago. "Listen, I'm late as it is. I gotta go. I'll call you tonight when it's over."

"You can tell me in person. I'll be there."

"Aw, shit, Reg. Tell me you don't plan on starting anything. Crashing the party isn't a good idea."

"No, I won't start anything. And I'm not crashing, either."

I stopped in my tracks. "Wait, what?"

"Camilla sent me an invitation. Weird, right? That's why I've got a bad feeling, kid. Just please don't play those songs."

I reassured him that everything would be fine and said goodbye, but Reggie's bad feeling was infectious and followed me into the shower. As I let the scalding water wash over me, I wondered what Camilla was up to. Why would she frame Reggie to keep him away, only to turn around and invite him to the show?

Looking back on it now, it all seems so obvious, but at the time I was too caught up in my own head to see the forest for the trees. As I got ready for the show, all I could think about was the dream I'd had, and my conversation with the faceless thing on the shore.

Just before I left to go downstairs to the lobby, I realized what I was going to say to that sickening creature.

"But I'm not wearing a mask," I whispered aloud. My hotel room offered no reply, and I left for the show a moment after.

There are some things about that night which have left my memory over the years. What Bobby and Hank were wearing, for example. Whenever I call up their images from my mental databank, I can see their faces just fine, but the rest of them are nondescript placeholders, as though their bodies have been swapped out for featureless mannequins.

I don't remember our limo driver's name. I don't remember what Reggie was wearing when I saw him working his way to the front of the bleeding crowd. My guitar tech's name escapes me—Wayne or Shawn or Mark, one of those three, but I'll be damned if I can pinpoint which.

I do remember how many people were there: 193 reporters, critics, and bloggers, including their plus-ones. If you want to consider the band, techs, roadies, and club staff, you're looking at another 41 people, for a total of 234 bodies inside that building. Sixteen people shy of its 250-person occupancy rating. 123 men and 111 women.

Out of those 234 people, 233 of them died that night in a variety of gruesome ways. Out of them all, I'm the only one who survived.

I can see by the way you're looking at me that you think my math is off. That there were 235 people in that club, not 234. That there were two survivors, not just one. Me and one other who may have escaped before the inferno consumed the building. The suspected arsonist, Camilla Bierce.

I stand by my statement: 234 people. Not 235. Adding an extra person to that number would imply Camilla's a human being.

Believe me, Mr. Hargrove, she was something much, much worse. She showed us her true nature after our show began. After the time came for everyone at our grand masquerade to take off their masks.

A lot of musicians will tell you that they never get over the pre-show jitters, and I was no exception. I always felt nauseated before a show, and my hands would shake until I picked up my guitar. You might say I depended on my Gibson for more than just music; I needed it to steady myself. I felt naked without it any time I was on a stage, getting ready to perform.

That night I felt the same pre-show trepidation, but it was tainted with a lingering fear at the nape of my neck and a hint of bile at the back of my throat. My mind had become a haunted house, filled with the rattling phantoms of Reggie's pleas and the faceless beings from Carcosa's shoreline. I tried to put those ceaseless worries out of my head for the next couple of hours. *Focus*, I told myself. *You've got a show to play. It'll be over before you know.*

We took to the stage while the curtain was down, dressed in the crimson robes of Camilla's choosing. Noise from the crowd filtered through the thick red fabric, transforming voices into soft murmurs, and I remember thinking they sounded a lot like the hiss of crashing waves.

The stage itself was fully decorated, our places marked with red duct tape according to Johnny's geometric diagram. An authentic throne, generously donated by one of Camilla's connections, stood center stage, draped in gold and red cloth. The statue of King Hastur from Camilla's apartment stood in front of it, its hidden face pointed toward the crowd. Black candles lined Bobby's drum set riser, flickering erratically, disturbed by our movement. The wall behind us was sheathed in golden drapery, and from the rafters hung a large plaque adorned with a golden symbol.

I recognized it immediately. The sign of Camilla's king. The Yellow Sign.

"I almost forgot!"

We turned toward the side of the stage. Camilla wore a red miniskirt with golden trim. I remember because of the way the colors complimented her eyes. They, too, were gold that night. She had a handful of what looked like red lanyards and handed one to each of us.

"Wear these tonight." She kissed me on the cheek. "For me. For luck. For the king."

At the end of the red ribbon was an onyx jewel, and carved into it was the shape of the same yellow symbol. I looked at it, puzzled. You know that weird feeling you get when you experience déjà vu? It was a lot like that, except it didn't carry the same weight of novelty. This was far heavier, pushing down on my soul with a kind of dread I'd never experienced before.

Camilla proceeded to kiss each of us on the cheek. Well, except for Johnny. She sucked face with him for a full minute before pulling away and wiping her lipstick from his lips.

"Do we have to do this?" Bobby looked at me, and then to Hank. Johnny turned toward us and nodded.

"Just for tonight, guys."

Hank said nothing, and he didn't have to. The roll of his eyes said all they needed to. We put our good luck charms over our heads, took to our instruments, and waited for our introduction.

Outside the curtain, Vinnie Klorso walked to the center of the stage, tapped the microphone, and addressed the crowd.

"Good evening, ladies and gentlemen. I want to thank you all for joining us tonight. The Hyades is proud to host The Yellow Kings for this limited engagement. Before we begin, the band has asked that you please wear the masks that were provided at the door. Go on, it's all in good fun."

Hushed murmurs followed Vinnie's request. As I'm sure you might have guessed, that request was made by Camilla. The Yellow Kings had nothing to do with it. It's one of the few things Johnny had a problem with, citing concerns that the crowd wouldn't be able to see us. Naturally, Camilla eased his mind and got her way.

A full minute passed before Vinnie spoke. "Excellent,

yes, very good. Thank you for participating. Now, on with the show. Ladies and gentlemen, it is my sincere honor to present to you The Yellow Kings and the Final Reconciliation."

A swell of cheers erupted from the crowd as the lights went out. I glanced over at Hank, then back to Bobby. Johnny walked forward and took his place behind the throne.

Bobby raised his drumsticks and counted us off.

"*One, two, three, four—*"

Johnny struck the first power chord of 'Reconciliatory Matters', let the crunch resonate across the crowd, and played a full measure until I took the lead. That first solo comes early in the song, and my fingers were on fire. As soon as my fingers slid across the fret, the curtains parted and the stage lights washed over us. For a moment I was blinded, but I didn't need to see. I was playing on pure muscle memory, hitting every note with perfect time, and when the flashing colors left my vision, I saw a sea of white masks staring back at us, all bobbing their heads in time to the music.

That first instrumental track lasts about two minutes, slowly building to a crescendo that transitions into the second song. Johnny walked out from behind the throne at just the right moment, strutting toward the microphone with his arms outstretched like a rock messiah. The crowd exploded with cheers.

Johnny took the microphone, clutched the stand, and leaned forward over the pit.

"*She waits beneath a dim sky at dusk,*" he sang, "*a wanderer out of harrowed time.*"

The response from the crowd was more than we'd expected. After weeks of stress and tension in the band, playing those first few songs really put us back at the heart of why we made music in the first place. I stole a glimpse at Hank and Bobby. They were both smiling.

There's something surreal and gratifying about taking something you've created in the womb of your own mind, presenting it to others, and watching them respond in a positive way. It's an addictive sensation, a chemical reaction wrought by our own minds, and perhaps the true reason artists create their art. Standing there on that stage in front of that small crowd of people took me back to the days when we played shows in Bobby's garage, charging the neighborhood kids a buck a piece to watch us perform. We'd used that money to bribe Hank's older brother into getting us a twelve-pack of beer.

Our music wasn't as raw as it was back then, but what it lacked in crude sound it more than made up for in power. Every note we hit that night had the force of a sucker punch. We didn't merely play those songs for the crowd; we attacked them, ripping into them like wild animals. We'd starved for weeks in that studio, and now we'd have our nourishment.

'Wanderer' transitioned into 'Dim Carcosa', and during Hank's bass-driven lead up, Johnny held out his hand to the crowd.

"How're you doin' tonight, Carcosa?"

The crowd cheered.

"I can't *hear* you, Carcosa!"

Their roar intensified.

I was too caught up in the music at the time, but it did occur to me later how those hapless people in the crowd reacted to the word 'Carcosa'. I've often wondered if they secretly knew of that golden city, or if they were caught up in the moment like we were. I suspect their indifference had everything to do with the latter. And who could blame them? We were fucking rocking the place.

The change began toward the end of the fourth song in our set. It may have started sooner than that, but the first time I noticed was during Bobby's synth solo at the end of

'Usurper'. Considering they were dressed in masks like the rest of the crowd, I guess they could've been there from the beginning. The members of Carcosa's congregation stared down at us from the balcony, the sleeves of their robes draped over the railing like drawn curtains. I'm not sure if the others noticed them. I spotted the comically large figures purely by chance, flicking my head to brush the hair out of my face.

My mouth went dry, and I wanted to stop what I was doing so I could alert my bandmates, but for some reason, I struck the opening notes of the next song. The air grew stale, warm, my lungs constricting as they withered into husks. I tried to move my legs, but they wouldn't cooperate, mired to the floor by an unseen bog. When I looked down, I discovered the red outline of Johnny's geometric design was glowing.

I blinked, held my breath, and then exhaled. The glow was still there, piercing and unnatural as though lit by a black light bulb, which was impossible because I knew our show employed no such thing. Still, my hands played, slaves to another master, and when I looked over at my bandmates, they seemed to be struggling with the same realizations. Only Johnny appeared unaffected, caught up in the majesty of his lyrics as he belted them to the crowd, a crazed bard come from afar to tell the tale of a strange traveler, a dark wanderer, and a usurper to the throne of a faceless king.

The world around us shimmered, flickering like heat on a horizon line, pulling back the curtain of one reality to reveal another. And I swear to you, as I live and breathe, that whole fucking club was transported to that dream-place on the darkened shoreline. When I craned my neck, we were no longer on a stage, but at the gates of Carcosa itself. Those cyclopean towers shot skyward at unnatural angles, looming over us like snaking vines ready to pluck us like the ants we were.

But still, we played. We played better than we'd ever played before. I looked down at my fingers and discovered they were bleeding, the calluses that had formed years ago ripped open and fresh once more. I tried to stop, but my muscles would not obey, and I craned back my neck to scream. Finally, I understood why Johnny wouldn't let us play more than three songs at a time. Whatever its purpose, this music was the catalyst. We were puppets, standing where we were told, playing the notes we were told. We four Yellow Kings were mere pawns placed precariously across Camilla's chessboard. And now the final moves were in play.

The crowd no longer bobbed or moved in time to our movement. They stood like lifeless puppets, their expressionless masks staring out toward us, toward the gates of the golden city.

Time transmuted into water, washing over us like the dark, briny tides of Hali. Toward the back of the club, or where the back of the club used to be, I glimpsed the twin moons rising over a horizon of churning waters, crossing a red sky peppered with blackened stars.

'Leech' bled into 'Stars', and on we played—slaves to our art. I felt my head lighten from the loss of blood, but no matter how hard I tried to tear my fingers away from the strings, they would not obey.

Let it happen, I heard Camilla whisper. *You want this*.

Her words shifted into Johnny's lyrics, their voices transposed over one another, and for a time I thought it was Camilla who was singing, or maybe it was Johnny whispering into my ear. Both had become one, two sides of the same damned coin, singing in shrill pitch to the darkening heavens above, swearing their oath to reconcile the kingdoms of Hastur.

I craned my neck to the side to check on Hank and Bobby. Hank stood in a crooked manner, his bass slung low almost to his knees, playing feverishly as he shook his head in time to the notes. At first, I thought he was caught up in the thrash of the song, but when we hit the end of the measurement, I could hear him screaming in agony. A dark stream of blood dripped down the side of his bass.

Bobby's eyes and nose bled. Every time he struck his snare, blood sprayed outward, caking his cymbals like a dark Pollock painting. He looked too exhausted to scream, had somehow grown older in the fifty minutes or so since the show began.

As 'Stars' segued into 'Masques', I caught sight of something that I'm still not certain actually happened. You would think that after everything I've told you, surely something as simple as this would be equally believable, but you must trust me, Mr. Hargrove—this is hard to swallow, even for me.

Camilla's statue of the faceless king moved. Slow, the fingers merely twitching, flexing, testing their constitution as bits of marble chipped and fell to the stage. The mask it held in its hand followed soon after and cracked down the center.

I played on, but I dared not take my eyes off that impossible thing. I opened my eyes to scream, but I'd burned out my lungs, my voice nothing more than dry hot air, the sound of sand in a desert gale. The statue closed its free hand into a fist, stretching its marble joints before flattening the thin, pale fingers to its face. With both hands together, Hastur buried his head into his palms and raked his stony fingers down the featureless palate of his face. Shreds of marble fell to the floor in powdery white clumps, accompanied by a deep, guttural scream that bellowed from deep beneath our bones.

Was I hallucinating? Did Bobby or Hank even see this happen? I don't know, and I never will.

I was so caught up in the horror of what I'd witnessed

that I missed Johnny's introduction to the title track, 'The Final Reconciliation'.

And finally, Mr. Hargrove, we come to the reason why you're here. What happened that night in the Hyades club? Everything I've told you these past few hours has all built up to this moment, and I find that my old heart is beating in my chest just as it did that night onstage. I can almost taste the blood on my tongue and smell the cinders burning in my nostrils.

And if I close my eyes, I can still hear Johnny singing—

"Your resistance to truth is vile / I don't need your repudiation / You can suffer in torment while / we call for the final reconciliation."

The song carried the same thrashing tempo of Slayer's 'Disciple' (which was Bobby's inspiration for the beat, if I recall), but we put our own progressive spin on it. Compared to the other songs on the album, 'Final Rec' as we called it was probably one of the tamer tracks as far as vocals go. Johnny sang the lines with the same baritone bravado as he did on the *Jesters in Our Court* EP.

"Under twin moons I give my life / I will untie the binding lines / I pray this blood will suffice / to honor his Yellow Sign."

The bridge gave way to the chorus, and Johnny unleashed his death metal growl like a surprise attack on the audience. We'd taken heat from prog metal 'purists' in the past who said we were too weak to stand up against the greats. Johnny must've taken that to heart because the clawing vitriol he spewed into the microphone for the chorus gave everyone pause.

I tell you this because the chorus was the beginning of the end. It's when all hell broke loose in the club.

Johnny raised one fist into the air and braced the microphone stand with the other. He squeezed so hard the color drained from his knuckles. Bobby paused for half a beat, Hank plucked three notes on his bass, and Johnny thrust his fist higher into the air.

"*Take off your mask!*"

A wave of uncertainty fluttered through the crowd. Another half-beat and up-strum of the bass. I stepped forward and depressed the wah-wah pedal, beginning my solo on the second refrain.

"*Take off your mask!*"

Johnny took hold of his guitar, moved up the fret, and together the four of us jammed the third refrain, a continuous battery of distortion and sonic murder. Finally, another pause and half-beat. The voice that crawled out of his throat wasn't his own, and it wasn't Camilla's, either. It was the voice of Hastur, the true Yellow King.

"*TAKE OFF YOUR MASK!*"

One by one, members of the audience tucked their fingers beneath the rims of their masks—and discovered they couldn't pull them off. Have you ever seen panic manifest itself in a crowd? It moves with erratic fervor, like a time-lapsed video of maggots working within a rotting carcass, one part of the animal twitching nervously, inflating like a balloon. before moving on to the next decayed organ.

One by one, the Yellow King's congregation pulled and scratched and clawed at their masks.

One by one, they extracted the pallid masks from their faces, revealing charred, blackened holes rimmed with writhing worms.

Everything from my nightmare unfolded before me in real time, and my fingers mercifully ceased their playing just as Hastur's corrupted voice boomed overhead.

"*TAKE OFF YOUR MASK!*"

Spent, my limbs drained of all feeling, and lightheaded from the blood loss, I staggered off my marker and into the side of Bobby's platform. The black candles tumbled off the edge, rolling with flickering flames into the side of the empty golden throne. I don't know what that antique chair was made of, but it went up in a whoosh of flames like dry kindling, interrupting Bobby's soft, exhausted piano solo of the final instrumental track.

I heard Hank drunkenly shout, "What the fuck?" But his voice was displaced by shrieks from the crowd. When I peered out from behind the pyre of flames on the stage, I glimpsed a tapestry of agony painted in deep, dark crimson.

My mind shut down for a moment. What I saw forced me into a reboot cycle. The hallucination was gone. The interior of the club had returned. Gone were the twin moons and sky. The towers of Carcosa had vanished. All that remained was our congregation screeching, writhing, rocked with spasms of pain I can only fathom.

They had done as Johnny had bade them. They'd taken off their masks. One by one they had torn into their flesh and pulled off their faces like old, tattered wallpaper. Glistening red faces peered back at each other in wide-eyed panic, each face a look of shock and surprise, their lipless mouths frozen forever in toothy smiles.

I staggered toward Johnny's place on the stage. He was leaning against the microphone stand, his shoulders rising and falling with deep, labored breaths. I don't know if he was still caught in the trance of the music. He was still wearing his shades.

"Johnny," I croaked, "brother, what the fuck did you do? What did *we* do?"

He mumbled something to himself, something I couldn't hear over the cries of the wounded in the crowd. Below us, I glimpsed one bloody soul working his way toward the stage, his face pulled down around his collar like a wet piece of cloth. I didn't recognize him at first—I mean, how could you recognize anyone without a face?— but as he neared us, I could make out his voice.

My heart sank. Reggie. My God, poor Reggie. He reached out to us, beckoning for us to save him, or maybe even to accuse us. These days I lean toward the latter. Why wouldn't he accuse us? He'd tried to warn me, tried to stop me from going onstage, and wasn't it just like old Reg to say "I told you so?"

Of course it was. That poor son of a bitch.

I watched him collapse in shock and looked away only when a panicked woman sank her heel into the wet viscera of his new face.

Johnny fell to his knees and yanked the shades from his face. He looked upon the mayhem wrought by his songs in a horrified daze. When I looked back, I saw the flames had spread from the throne to the drapery behind the stage, filling the room with a devilish orange glow.

Hank dropped his bass and had taken two steps toward us when Camilla rushed him. She moved like an animal, leaping onto his back and throwing off his center of balance. He fell to the stage with a tired yelp as Camilla jammed her knees into his spine.

"*Unmask,*" she screeched, grabbing a fistful of his hair. "*Unmask, you filth!*"

I met Hank's gaze in the moment before she tore out his eyes. He had no idea what was happening. I like to think it's better that he didn't. When Camilla's nails sank into his eyelids and the screaming started, I had to look away. I don't care if that makes me a coward. I just couldn't watch my friend be eviscerated by that witch.

The flames climbed the drapery behind us with alarming speed, shooting up to the rafters and spilling across the ceiling in roiling waves. By the time I remembered Bobby, I was already too late to do anything to save him. He'd collapsed over his synth. I'll never know if he was alive or dead when the fire swept over him. Considering how he'd fainted over his drum kit weeks before in the studio, I like to believe his heart just couldn't take the stress and had simply given out.

I know better, of course, but this lie helps me sleep better. Not by much, but better.

"Oh, Aidan." Camilla rose to her feet and hovered over the stage. Her eyes burned with gold, illuminating the cracks along her face with a sickening light. Blood and viscera fell from her hands in thick, wet clumps. "Won't you take off your mask?"

She floated toward me. I braced myself for the end, for the inevitable pain that must come from feeling one's flesh ripped from bone.

And in the end, it was Johnny who saved me. Johnny Leifthauser, my lonely schoolyard friend. The quiet nerd who scribbled poetry in his notebook. The founder of The Yellow Kings.

As I closed my eyes to meet my fate, Johnny stepped between us. "That's enough from you, bitch."

My heart leapt into my throat. Blood dribbled out of Johnny's eyes, but when he glanced at me and smiled, I saw that it was *him* in there. The real Johnny. The one who'd fallen under Camilla's spell months before.

"Aww, Johnny, come on." Camilla's face was a glowing ball of gold now, her skin peeling and cracking like old paint, the façade slowly melting away. Short, gray nubs protruded through the openings in her skin, seeking the air, tasting it. "I thought we were in love?"

Johnny gripped the neck of his Fender and swung the guitar, striking Camilla across the face. The blow removed her mask in three large chunks of flesh. Golden light leaked out of the withered hole in her skull, illuminating the mass of worms crawling along the rim.

"Get out of here," Johnny said.

A low, rumbling hiss erupted from the gaping hole in Camilla's unmasked face. "*It's your turn, lover. Time to take off your mask and reconcile with the true king in yellow.*"

My legs refused to move. I gaped in horror at the impossible creature standing before us.

"Go, goddammit!" Johnny shoved me off the stage. I landed hard on the floor, and the impact drove the air out of me. "Go be someone else's pain in the ass!"

That's the last thing Johnny ever said to me. As I struggled to take that next precious gasp of air, the thing that was Camilla Bierce descended upon my friend and tore out his throat.

Panicked, I sought my way along the mass of fallen bodies, sinking my hands into their exposed faces. I stayed as low as possible, as the smoke from the raging inferno had filled the room with a darkening haze. The last memory I have of that night is turning back to glimpse Camilla's glowing figure kneeling before the statue of her faceless king.

"No mask?" Her scream echoed through the room, overpowering the roar and crackle of flames. "*No mask!*"

TRACK #9
TATTERS OF THE KING

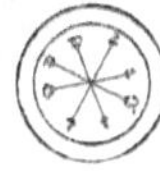

The old rock star smoked his last cigarette down to the filter and slumped back in his seat. To Miles, he looked like an old worn-out doll, his days of bringing joy to children far behind him. Over the last few hours he'd watched life return to Aidan Cross's eyes, only to fizzle and fade yet again as the old man recounted his band's triumphs, failures, and untimely demise. Although he would never admit it to his crew, the story spooked Miles Hargrove to his core. He'd read the official police report from all those years ago, and he'd grown up hearing the rumors of ritual activity on the night of the final show, but to hear a first-hand account by someone who was there was soul-crushing.

"So what happened after that?" Miles asked.

Aidan Cross placed the smoldering cigarette filter into the ashtray with the others. He cleared his throat. "About what you'd expect, I guess. They found me on the curb outside the club, unconscious and nearly dead from smoke inhalation. The Hyades club burned to the ground. Last I heard, they'd built a fucking Starbucks in its place. So much for respect for the dead."

Miles nodded. "You're right, they did." He scribbled something on his notepad. "And after?"

"Ah yes, after. There were police inquiries and lawyers and reporters like yourself. All of them wanted the scoop, to understand what had happened, and more importantly, why. They all wanted to know about what sort of drugs we were doing, what we'd been drinking, who Camilla was. That last point of interest was the most perplexing, you see. The most troubling."

"How so?"

Aidan smirked. "You even have to ask? No one had ever heard of Camilla Bierce. That fancy loft apartment of hers, with all her occult shit, was registered in someone else's name. Cassilda-something. Her mother, I think, but I could be wrong about that."

"My notes do say Cassilda Pulver, but all I have is a name. Records say she was deceased long before the fire at the club."

"Yeah, something like that. She'd been dead for years. Decades. The only person who could shed any light on who Camilla was, was Camilla herself." Aidan folded his arms and stared at the table between them. "All of her secrets died with her."

"And you never played guitar again?"

Aidan shook his head. "I tried for a while, but my heart just wasn't in it anymore. After what I'd done to those poor souls with these things—" He held up his hands, wrinkled and knotted with arthritis. "—how could I even dream of picking up my Fender again?"

Miles offered a nod of sympathy. "Of course. You mentioned attorneys a moment ago. I believe your legal troubles following the incident were well-documented. If you'd prefer not to discuss—"

"No, no, that's fine. Most of those vultures are dead by now anyway." Aidan chuckled dryly, a raspy scoff that sounded like a choking dog. "Since I was the only remaining member of the band, all the families of everyone who died in the club—including Bobby's and Hank's parents—came after me. At the end of the day, I never saw another dime of royalties from sales of our EP. And the album, of course, was never released to the public, so…" Aidan finished his sentence with a tired shrug. "I took up a few jobs here and there to make ends meet. I did that for some years until my accident."

The producer shifted uncomfortably in his seat. He'd spent the last several hours avoiding the topic of Aidan's facial scars, but now they were front and center. "Yes, I suppose I need to ask you about that unfortunate incident. We can keep this brief if you prefer."

"I don't mind," said the old man. "To be honest, there isn't much to tell. I believe the official report said 'survivor's guilt', and I guess, in some ways, they aren't wrong about that. It eats me up inside, knowing that what we did that night caused so much agony. Every time I close my eyes to sleep, I find myself back up on that stage, with Carcosa's towers looming over us, and the red congregation chanting back at us in time to that damned music. The dream always goes on forever, to the point where Johnny chants for them to take off their masks, and I have to relive watching them mutilate themselves all over again. Almost every night I have this awful nightmare. You can ask the nurses.

"Anyway, one night a few years back, while in the throes of one of these night terrors, I decided I'd join the congregation and punish myself along with them. I was living with a roommate at the time—old Marcus Norton, God rest his soul—and I woke him up with my screaming. By the time Marcus was able to restrain me, I'd already done the worst of this." Aidan fanned out his fingers and traced the tips along the deep ridges carved into his cheeks. Miles observed for the first time just how neat and trim the old rocker's fingernails were. "That's how I ended up in here, you know. They thought I was a suicide risk and committed me for observation. Apparently, I still cry out to Carcosa in my sleep. That led to more questions, which led to more observation, and then they decided to keep me for good. For my health, you see."

A heavy silence fell between them, and for a few moments, Miles feared the old man had fallen asleep. The dark sunglasses on the old man's face obscured his eyes a little too well. Miles caught Jody's eye and shrugged. Finally, when Miles leaned forward to wake him, Aidan held up his hand in protest. "I'm still with you, Mr. Hargrove. Forgive me, my mind wanders sometimes."

Miles smiled. "That's quite all right. Penny for your thoughts?"

"I was just thinking about this." Aidan reached into his pocket and extracted a coiled silver chain. Nested in the center was a dark onyx jewel. Miles recognized it from the old man's story, following it with his eyes as the chain swayed to-and-fro like a pendulum. The years had not dulled the golden trim of the pendant's insignia. Miles motioned for Jody to zoom in on the object, and the cameraman did so.

"Here." The old rock star placed the onyx jewel on the table and slid it toward the interviewer. "For you. My last fan."

Miles Hargrove's eyes lit up with a ravenous delight, betraying the forced frown spreading across his face. He balked at the gesture, shaking his head. "Oh, no, Mr. Cross, I couldn't possibly take—"

"Please, save me that horseshit. I've held on to it for far too long, and it's the least I could do for letting me ramble on all these hours." Aidan turned away and peered over his shoulder into the darkened corner of the room. He took off his shades. "Isn't it about time for my meds, Diane?"

One of the nurses waiting near the door nodded to him. "Yes, Mr. Cross. You'll be needing your medication soon." Diane turned her attention to Mr. Hargrove. "Just a few more minutes, please."

Miles rolled the onyx stone over his hands, running his thumb across the golden insignia. He felt impossibly giddy to be given such a gift, a true piece of rock and roll memorabilia. An actual pendant worn by one of the Yellow Kings on the night of their final show. It could be worth a fortune. No, better yet, it was priceless.

Nurse Diane cleared her throat. "Mr. Hargrove?"

"Yes," he said. "I'm sorry. Yes, we'll wrap this up in just a few minutes." He skimmed his notes and fell upon the scribbling of words he'd written an hour before. "I do have one more question, Mr. Cross."

Aidan turned back in his seat and placed his hands on the table. "Shoot."

"A little while ago you talked about Bobby asking Johnny what it all meant, and Johnny sort of brushed off the question. You said you'd pieced it together yourself but never got around to explaining it to them. Do you mind sharing that with us?"

Smiling, Aidan Cross leaned back and tilted his head up to the light. He squinted and took a deep breath.

"Actually, Mr. Hargrove, I think I do mind. That album was put together to drive men mad, to fill their heads with visions of something we aren't meant to see. Knowledge of something we aren't meant to know. David Reiflen, the owner of the record label, told me he'd personally see to the destruction of the album masters. Swore to me he'd burn them himself. No, Miles, I'd prefer we leave their scattered ashes alone."

"But…"

"I've made up my mind on that, sir. Please don't badger me. I'm an old man and I don't need the grief."

"No," Miles said, "that's fine, I just… I'm surprised no one told you."

The color drained from Aidan's face. "Told me what?"

"Did you not understand why we came to you today?

The record company hired us to interview you for the 50th anniversary of the recording. The album…" Miles Hargrove's throat clicked when he swallowed. "The album's being released for the first time later this year."

Aidan sank back in his chair. The air slipped out of the room, and for the longest of seconds, still silence took its place.

A moment later, the screaming started.

Miles Hargrove watched Jody pack up the camera equipment into the back of the van. After the doors slammed shut, Jody stepped back and scowled at the producer. "Fuck, man, why'd you have to set him off like that? Hasn't he been through enough?"

"Hey, that wasn't planned. Honest. I really thought he knew why we were there."

Jody shook his head in disgust. "Whatever, man. I'll see you back at the hotel."

Miles nodded, looking back at the sleek black limousine waiting in the facility parking lot. "Sure thing," he whispered. As Jody drove away, Miles reached into his pocket and took out the black pendant the old man gave him. He lifted it before his face and stared transfixed at the curved golden insignia.

He was so entranced by its beauty that he didn't hear the limousine's back door open, or the clap of one high heel on the pavement.

"Whatcha got there, handsome?"

Miles turned back and smiled at the auburn-haired beauty leaning against the side of the limo. He approached her with the pendant stretched out before him, an offering to his goddess.

"A gift, my love."

The woman smiled, illuminating her eyes, which were two different colors. One brown, one hazel, and sometimes gold. Her coquettish gaze lit upon the onyx jewel.

She smiled. "Have you found the Yellow Sign?"

THE END

 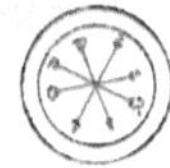  

AFTERWORD:
NO SMILING
IN ROCK 'N ROLL

There was a point in my youth when my parents thought I'd sold my soul to the devil. I was sixteen at the time, still in the early stages of figuring out who I was, where I fit in the grand scheme, and who I wanted to be. I wasn't a social butterfly, but I did have a small network of friends—other weirdos and geeks who didn't fit in with the status quo—and they all seemed to have their "thing." This person was really into *this* band, or that person was really into *that* activity. At that age, when you're trying to figure out who you are, you tend to make things like this your whole personality. It's how you identify and signal to others that this is what you're about. For me, it was a black T-shirt.

The date: September 9th, 1999. Three things happened: the music video for "We're In This Together" by Nine Inch Nails debuted on MTV. Afterward, an interview with Kurt Loder and Trent Reznor. And after that, Nine Inch Nails performed "The Fragile" during the MTV Video Music Awards. Right time, right place, right as I was supposed to be studying for a test the following day, I was glued to the TV as a pasty-pale Trent Reznor took the stage and began singing the slow, somber intro. And when the band hit the song's crescendo, the guitar solo kicked in and the intensity began to climb, I felt an electrical surge in my limbs, my heart, an emotional connection I'd never felt with music before.

The rest is history. I became a fan for life.

And the black T-shirt, well, it's not what you'd expect. It wasn't emblazoned with the NIN logo; it wasn't even a band shirt. It caught my eye a couple of months later while browsing the bins at Soundtrax, my hometown's only record store. "Evil," it read. In sparkly letters against plain black fabric. I had to have it.

My parents hadn't noticed the shift in my musical taste, but they definitely noticed the change in wardrobe.

"Why are you wearing black all of a sudden?"

"What's wrong with you? You can't wear that to church."

"You never smile anymore."

And I didn't have an answer then, nor was I capable of articulating one. It was a feeling. Like I'd found myself, or at least a path toward finding myself, but for an introverted, autistic sixteen-year-old, putting that into words seemed impossible. All I had to explain myself was *The Fragile,* NIN's double album, which tapped into all those things I couldn't say. My parents weren't interested in listening, and to be honest, I don't think it would've mattered anyway. What they saw was a sudden tonal shift in their kid's personality. I stopped going to church, stopped spending time with them, stopped doing the things that I'd never felt comfortable doing.

Because the music made me confident. I felt more comfortable with being who I wanted to be. The music conveyed a similar rage, desperation, and sadness I felt bubbling below my skin every single day. It told me I wasn't alone in feeling the way I did, and that it was okay not to wear a mask every day. I didn't feel the pressure to smile so much anymore—because I really wasn't happy in my own skin, in my home, or at school. I was being truer to myself, and the real me, the one who emerged after this great awakening, really didn't want to smile. It was okay to feel angry. It was okay to frown. It was okay to feel all those negative emotions. And fuck everyone else who had a problem with it.

This may seem obvious now, and it is, but back then it was a revelation to a sheltered sixteen-year-old child. Listening to Nine Inch Nails brought me out of a shell I didn't know I had, and opened doors to worlds inside my head.

The following year, I wrote my first novel, set to the soundtrack of NIN's *The Downward Spiral*. I've been writing to music ever since, and later this year, I plan to revisit that first novel and rewrite it for a modern audience. I expect the music of Nine Inch Nails will be playing in the background once again. In fact, I guarantee it.

I wrote everything above to say this with regard to *The Final Reconciliation*: I tried to tap into that joy I felt that day back in '99. The energy, the angst, the emotion of it all. I know I got some things wrong on the technical side, but I admit the accuracy was secondary to the feeling.

Writing about Aidan's journey and the downfall of The Yellow Kings reconnected me with the satisfaction of creation. This novella ended an eighteen-month dry spell and served as the kick in the ass I needed, and in the years since, it's safe to say it revitalized my career. No, that's not quite true. This novella brought my writing career back from the dead, and writing it was like putting on the "Evil" shirt for the first time again.

It felt right. It felt dangerous and fun.

And to a thirty-something stuck in a corporate accounting job, it felt like permission to drop the mask I had to wear five days a week. It's been over a decade since I first had the idea, nearly a full decade since this book was originally published, and I still haven't picked up that mask.

In closing, I'll share this anecdote. My manager once pulled me into a one-on-one meeting and told me I made people uncomfortable because I didn't smile. I didn't have a measured response for him then, but I do now. It's something Trent Reznor told Rob Sheridan, the band's visual designer for over a decade, with regard to posing for photographs: "There's no smiling in rock 'n roll."

Todd Keisling
Womelsdorf, Pennsylvania
April 10th, 2025

 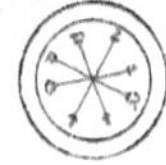  

ACKNOWLEDGMENTS

The folks who know me best know I love music: Everything I write has a soundtrack. Hell, my first novel wouldn't exist if not for the music of Nine Inch Nails. But that's a different story, a different time, and a different genre. *This* story, however, wouldn't exist without the support and encouragement of a few rock stars I'm blessed to know.

Many thanks to Joe Mynhardt at Crystal Lake for taking a chance on a weirdo like me. I'm grateful to say Joe's more than just my publisher—he's also a good friend and a fellow metal head.

A huge, heartfelt thanks goes to my editors, Amelia Bennett and Monique Snyman, for providing their surgical expertise and excising all the bad parts. They made the story better, with minimal scarring.

My dear friends Mercedes M. Yardley, Anthony J. Rapino, Eryk Pruitt, Nikki Nelson-Hicks, and Brian Kirk all offered much-needed feedback at various stages of this story's development. They are excellent writers, and I urge you to check out their work. They're my tribe and I love them dearly.

Special recognition is owed to my friends Michael Auchenbach and Chad Lutzke for providing technical assistance with various aspects of musicianship, from studio arrangement to recording terminology. If I got anything right, it's because of them. Technical errors are mine alone.

A number of friends taught me everything I know about metal, and I'd be remiss if I didn't mention them here: 'Psycho' Larry Hale, Josh Jones, Gvid Brown, David Rockey, Jason Brafford, John Brittain, Daniel Klein, and Mike Mollura. They introduced me to the work of Nine Inch Nails, Tool, A Perfect Circle, Opeth, Slayer, Pantera, Type O Negative, and countless others. I'm forever in their debt.

Above all, though, my love and gratitude to Erica and Gabe. Erica is my first reader and critic. She's never been wrong about one of my stories, so I was nervous when I gave her this one. "It's different," I told her. "You may not like it." She read it in one sitting and told me it's her favorite. Thanks, love. I needed that.

And now we've come to the end, so before we lower the curtain, let's all raise our lighters and throw up the devil horns. Thank you and goodnight!

Todd Keisling
Womelsdorf, Pennsylvania
8/19/14 – 1/11/17

TODD KEISLING is the two-time Bram Stoker Award®-nominated author of *Devil's Creek, Scanlines, Cold, Black & Infinite,* and most recently, *The Sundowner's Dance,* among several others. A pair of his earlier works were recipients of the University of Kentucky's Oswald Research & Creativity Prize for Creative Writing (2002 and 2005), and his second novel, *The Liminal Man,* was an Indie Book Award finalist in Horror & Suspense (2013). He lives in Pennsylvania with his family.

SHARE HIS DREAD
Bluesky: @toddkeisling.com
Instagram: @toddkeisling
www.toddkeisling.com

CONTENT WARNING

This story contains depictions of (or references to) the following: self-mutilation, sexual assault, sexual situations, rape (implied), misogyny, alcohol and drug abuse (implied), grief, the occult, ritualistic human sacrifice, and familial trauma.

www.ingramcontent.com/pod-product-compliance
Lightning Source LLC
Chambersburg PA
CBHW031054310726
48969CB00007B/2274